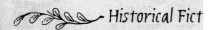 

Historical Fict

Liberty's Son
A Spy Story of the American Revolution

Paul B. Thompson

 Enslow Publishers, Inc.
40 Industrial Road
Box 398
Berkeley Heights, NJ 07922
USA

http://www.enslow.com

For Sara Irene

Copyright © 2010 by Paul B. Thompson

Library of Congress Cataloging-in-Publication Data:

Thompson, Paul B.
    Liberty's son : a spy story of the American Revolution / Paul B. Thompson.
        p. cm. — (Historical fiction adventures (HFA))
    Summary: In 1773, seventeen-year-old apothecary Oliver Carter moves to Boston and begins helping the Sons of Liberty in their rebellion against British tyranny in the colonies as well as discovering that his boss, Dr. Benjamin Church, is a traitor to the cause.
    ISBN-13: 978-0-7660-3309-2
    ISBN-10: 0-7660-3309-0
    [1. Pharmacists—Fiction. 2. Boston (Mass.)—History—Colonial period, ca. 1600–1775—Fiction. 3. Spies—Fiction. 4. Church, Benjamin, 1734–1778—Fiction. 5. Boston Tea Party, 1773—Fiction.] I. Title.
    PZ7.T3719828Li 2009
    [Fic]—dc22   2008040345

Paperback ISBN 978-0-7660-3654-3
Printed in China
012012 Leo Paper Group, Heshan City, Guangdong, China

10 9 8 7 6 5 4 3 2

This is a work of juvenile fiction.

Illustration Credits: Library of Congress, pp. 156, 158; Office of Medical History/ Office of the Surgeon General, p. 157; Original Painting by © Corey Wolfe, p. 1.

Cover Illustration: Original Painting by © Corey Wolfe.

Contents

Strong Medicine

June 1772

Providence, first city of His Majesty's colony of Rhode Island, had several apothecary's shops. The newest of these was Hargrave's Practical Chemist by the river. Harris Hargrave had come to Providence in 1770. His prices were low and the quality of his medicines high, thanks to his apprentice, Oliver Carter. As time went by, Hargrave applied himself more to land speculation than pharmacy, which he more and more left in the hands of his young employee. After two years, Harris Hargrave had all but vanished from the town's recollection, but everyone knew "young Carter the Chemist."

In June, the sun set late on Narragansett Bay, and night did not fully fall until after nine o'clock. As long as light lasted, there was work to do.

The shop was closed. Oliver had swept the floor, shut and latched the door, and was trying to fill the final prescriptions of the day. The orders common ones: essence of chamomile, sulfured molasses, and two dozen lavender pills for Mrs. Whipple, the merchant's wife. Pills were Oliver's specialty. He rolled the hardest, neatest pills in the colony— quite an accomplishment for a seventeen-year-old apprentice.

By the failing light, Oliver wrote the labels for the two bottles of liquid. His handwriting was very fine, as readable as copperplate. When he finished the labels, he opened the pill roller. It was hinged along one edge, like a book, and once apart revealed neat rows of pale pink pills. He tested every one, squeezing them between his thumb and forefinger. If a pill snapped or crumbled, Oliver put the remains back in the mortar and ground them again. Half the batch failed his pinch test. By the time he was done regrinding the broken pills, darkness had fallen.

Oliver lit a candle. The wick had just glowed to life when the front doorknob rattled hard. Startled, Oliver almost knocked over the light. Was it a clumsy night watchman or was it a thief, testing for unlocked doors? He waited, but the shaking was not repeated.

A loud knock sounded on the door, making the reversible "Open" and "Closed" sign dance on its hook. Arming himself with the hardwood pestle, Oliver went to the door. He listened. In the street, he could hear subdued voices.

"Who goes there?" he called in a hush.

"Free men all."

Hearing the correct watchword, Oliver unbolted the door and opened it a crack. Shadowed figures filled the lane.

"You that love liberty, join us!" said a low voice.

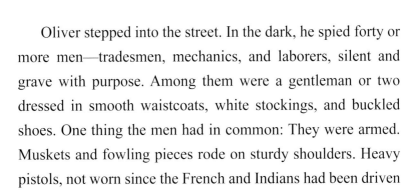

Oliver stepped into the street. In the dark, he spied forty or more men—tradesmen, mechanics, and laborers, silent and grave with purpose. Among them were a gentleman or two dressed in smooth waistcoats, white stockings, and buckled shoes. One thing the men had in common: They were armed. Muskets and fowling pieces rode on sturdy shoulders. Heavy pistols, not worn since the French and Indians had been driven from New England, weighted down the sashes of the better-dressed men. Those who did not own a gun carried old swords or even hatchets.

"Who's this boy?" someone asked.

"That's Carter," said the man leading the column. "He's with us, aren't you, Oliver?"

"I am, sir."

"Have you arms? No? Come along anyway. We'll find you something."

Under his tricorn hat, Oliver could see the leader's face was smeared with lampblack. This excited him more than the guns and blades displayed around him. In these dangerous times, many went about armed, but men only blackened their faces when they didn't want to be recognized. It was a sure sign dangerous deeds were afoot.

"Where are we going?"

"Ask not, but follow." The apothecary's apprentice turned away to reenter the shop. One of the men grabbed his arm.

"I must put my work away," Oliver protested.

"No one breaks ranks once we've begun," said the leader. "There's too great a chance of treachery."

Now he was alarmed. "What do you intend?" Oliver said, stepping back.

The gentleman laughed. "This is an Indian raid, can't you see? We are a Narragansett war party!"

Some of the men laughed. Most of them had red or black color on their faces. Not one was a true Indian.

"The pills I was making are for your wife, sir," Oliver said.

The gentleman considered. "Time is short." His wife's needs would have to wait. "Others are already on their way. We don't want to be the last ones there."

"They might start without us!" said another man. Some of the 'Indians' laughed again.

"All right," said Oliver. "At least let me lock the door."

He fished out the black iron key he wore on a string around his neck. It was dark, and his hands were shaking. Oliver fumbled with the long key, twice failing to get it in the lock. A burly man peered over his shoulder. "You're shaking like a wet dog. Maybe you should stay here."

"I'm going. I am a liberty man, same as any of you."

The gentleman planted his fists on his hips, revealing a brace of fine pistols in his belt. "Let him be, Daniel. Lock up, boy. We must not tarry too long."

Quietly they marched to the riverfront. Oliver saw a crowd of men already there, commandeering boats along the quay. Half of the band he had come with moved quickly into the

7

nearest longboat and rowed swiftly away from the pier. Oliver held the mooring taut as the rest of his companions climbed into another craft. He found himself in the stern holding a long-barreled fowling piece owned by a man now swinging an oar. The gun was primed and loaded.

Other boats were crawling across the bay around them. Six assorted small craft, heavily laden with armed men, had pulled away from shore ahead of Oliver's boat. He glanced back and saw one other boat leave the Pawtuxet shore behind them. No one raised sail but bent their backs to the sweeps.

With six oars in the water and two men on each oar, they soon caught up to the other boats.

"Where are we bound?" Oliver asked.

"You know Namquit Point?" the gentleman said. Oliver nodded. "That is our destination."

It was past eleven o'clock. They pulled hard against the tide, matching their speed to the rest of the little fleet. Before long, Oliver made out the dark outline of a ship on the horizon. It was a schooner with her sails furled and the lamps on her stern lit.

The gentleman took out a silver flask, pulled the cork with his teeth, and took a swig. He passed the flask to the sailor on the tiller. In the faint starlight, Oliver glimpsed an elaborate monogram etched in the silver.

"There she is," the steersman said in a loud whisper. Sound carried over water, especially on a calm night like this. The ship was only a mile away. A goodly vessel, she sat motionless on the calm sea. At first, Oliver thought she was anchored, but seeing the awkward slant of her leeward rail he realized she was hard aground.

A smuggler's ship, he reckoned, gone aground on the Point—a notorious spot. All the local packet boats marked it well, but a merchantman of that size must have come all the way from the West Indies. Liberty men of Providence and Pawtuxet had turned out to help land the cargo before the king's men could catch them.

"Are we landing a cargo?" Oliver asked breathlessly.

The hard-eyed sailor on the tiller gave him a sidelong glance. The well-dressed gentleman, face blackened like a chimney sweep, shook his head gravely.

"That's HMS *Gaspee*, King George's revenue cutter for the colony of Rhode Island."

Gaspee? Boatloads of armed men were making for a royal warship? Oliver looked again at the steadily growing silhouette of the stranded ship.

"You mean to tow her off?"

"I mean to send her to hell," was the harsh reply.

The boats gathered off the schooner's bow. Swells rocked the longboats, but the Royal Navy schooner was stuck on the bar. There was a hasty conversation between boats, as the leaders of each craft confirmed their plan one last time.

A man in a light-colored jersey appeared at the *Gaspee*'s rail. Spying the boats, he hailed them.

"Who comes here?" he shouted.

No one answered. Liberty men traded oars for guns as their weapons were passed forward. The sailor called again. Oliver's fowler was taken from him by its owner, crouching at the bow of the longboat.

Presently another man appeared on deck. He, too, wore a white shirt. In a high, angry voice he demanded once more, "Who comes here?"

The gentleman seated across from Oliver rose and shouted back, "I am the sheriff of the county of Kent!" He punctuated his declaration with some choice profanity, then continued, "I have a warrant to apprehend you, so surrender!"

The second man, whom Oliver understood to be the schooner's captain, replied with some oaths of his own. When he did, the burly steersman raised his musket and fired. The shot flashed as white as lightning. At once, the captain spun away and vanished below the rail. In the boats, the men gave a hurrah and swarmed up the sides of the schooner.

A hatchet was thrust into Oliver's hand. While the boarders scrambled up *Gaspee*'s side, Oliver stared in wonder at the battle unfolding before him. He believed in liberty and free trade for all colonists, but he had not expected to have to storm a Royal Navy warship to prove it.

"Come on!" called the last man in the boat. Breaking out of his daze, Oliver hurried forward, holding the gunwale with one hand to keep from being pitched into the sea. By the time he reached *Gaspee*'s deck the "Indian" raiders controlled the vessel.

"Where's the captain? Where's Dudingston?" the sharply dressed gentleman from Oliver's boat roared. Some rough-necks dragged a sailor up through a hatch and repeated the question.

"Shot, sir! Dying, seems like!" said the wide-eyed sailor.

"Carter! Come here!"

Oliver dropped the hatchet. He felt ridiculous holding it, since he could never strike anyone with such a thing. He was told to see to the wounded captain. With another liberty man named Mawney, he hurried to the commander's cabin. Bursting in, they found the ship's officer sitting on his bunk trying to stanch the flow of blood from a wound in his belly. He raised a cocked pistol, but Mawney snatched it from him before he could fire.

"I am Lieutenant William Dudingston, Royal Navy," he gasped. "If you mean to murder me, at least know my name!"

"No one's here to murder you," Mawney said. He was a medical student and quickly set to bandaging the lieutenant's wound. Oliver searched through the cupboard above the captain's bunk and found some drugs. He poured a dram of opiate and offered it to Dudingston. White-faced with pain, the Royal Navy officer refused it.

"I know your face," he whispered. "You'll hang for this!" Taken from the door of his shop without any warning, Oliver had not blackened his features.

"Quiet!" Mawney snapped. "If you live, remember this boy and I saved your life."

Men filled the doorway. "Out with him!" they cried. Oliver and Mawney held Dudingston between them and carried him out on deck.

"You'll seize no more honest men's ships!" declared another leader of the raiders, shaking his fist under the lieutenant's nose. "Nor impound any more cargoes or send good seamen to jail!"

"I did my duty to the king and to the law," Dudingston answered weakly. "The same law that will see you all dangling from the gallows!"

"Away with him!"

Gaspee's commander was hauled to a longboat. The rest of the crew, hands bound with cord, were taken off in other boats.

"Get going, the rest of you!" said Oliver's leader. A few liberty men lingered. One of the lamps on the stern was struck off and carried amidships, where its amber glow highlighted the faces of everyone left on board.

"Be off with you, Carter. Things are going to get hot here!"

In moments, *Gaspee* was ablaze. She burned to the waterline, destroyed for daring to enforce the king's laws.

Lieutenant Dudingston survived his wound. Before the week was out, Oliver Carter fled Providence so the vengeful officer could not make good his threat to introduce young Oliver to a hangman's noose.

chapter one

End of the Road

May 1773

I*need new shoes.* That was Oliver Carter's first thought as he topped the hill and saw the city of Boston for the first time. He had walked a long way, and his shoes were just about done in. The soles were thin as paper, and the square toes on each shoe were scuffed gray. Through the worn leather, he could see the big toe on each foot flexing. Good thing his journey was almost over. His pockets were empty. He had no money left to pay a cobbler to mend his shoes, but work and money awaited in Boston. In his pocket was a letter of introduction to a prominent Boston physician. The doctor needed a new apothecary, and Oliver needed a job.

He had walked most of the way from Manhattan. From time to time, friendly teamsters had given Oliver a ride. His longest hitch was a hay wagon in Connecticut that had lasted a whole day. Other than these few favors, his legs had carried him many miles.

He was taller than the average fellow, with wide shoulders and large hands. The mark of his Scots-Irish ancestors was in

13

his rusty red hair, gray eyes, and the spray of russet freckles that began on one cheek, passed over his long, sharp nose, and ended on his other cheek.

At eighteen, Oliver had been on his own for six years. His parents died of smallpox when he was twelve. Apprenticed in Philadelphia to an apothecary, he had learned the trade of mixing medicines at an early age. Now he was a journeyman, with papers proving his experience. Another six years' work and he could earn his master's papers. With those in hand, he could open a shop of his own.

Oliver sat down on the side of the road. He pulled off his fragile shoes and set them aside, then rolled down his stained stockings. Oliver was still wringing dew out of them when some horsemen cantered by, coming out from Boston. They were gentlemen all, each man accompanied by a servant also on horseback. Oliver counted eighteen men, a good sign. Eighteen riders leaving Boston the day eighteen-year-old Oliver Carter was arriving.

Cheered by this omen, he drew on his stockings, damp or not. His tattered shoes would survive another mile or two. Oliver took up his walking stick. Tied to it was a cloth bundle containing all his worldly possessions. He shouldered his modest burden and started down the hill.

The peninsula was called Boston Neck. Off to the right he had his first glimpse of the harbor. Oliver had heard in New York that Boston was really an island connected to the mainland by a slender peninsula.

More people joined him on the road. Many were on foot, but quite a few traveled by cart. They were tradesmen bound for the city markets with all sorts of goods—pottery, baskets, cured meats, and spring produce. Oliver saw quite a few wooden casks marked "Rum." Every town on the mainland ringing Boston had its own distillery where molasses from the West Indies was made into rum. The liquor then made its way back to the port of Boston, where it was shipped to every point in America and the Caribbean.

Traffic thickened near the fortified city gate. Day laborers grunted under hods of brick. Tailors and tinkers wove their barrows in and out of slower-moving tradesmen, eager to reach their customers before their competitors. Oliver paused at the rampart guarding the road, now called Orange Street. Gazing at the roofs and chimneys of Boston town, Oliver was lost in thought until a barrow man bumped him from behind.

"Look alive there, lad! This is no place for idle mooning!"

He ducked aside. A pushcart piled high with hay rattled by. Oliver dug out his letter of introduction. His benefactor in New York had inscribed the outside with the name: *Dr. Church, Hanover Street, Boston.* Hanover Street was on the north side of town, a good two miles away. With an eye to his failing footwear, Oliver trudged on.

Oliver arrived on Saturday, a market day, which accounted for the throng in the streets. He was no stranger to crowds, but Boston seemed more crowded than New York or Philadelphia. Perhaps because the streets were narrower and the buildings closer. He kept to the road, even though it changed names every few blocks. Orange Street became Newbury, then Marlborough, then Cornhill Street. Where Cornhill crossed King Street a square opened, dominated by a large church on the west side, and the Towne House in the center. Once the seat of the colony's government, the Towne House had also been a barrack for the redcoats. After the terrible events of 1770, when angry soldiers fired on a Boston mob, all the redcoats were removed from the city and posted to Castle William, on an island in the harbor.

Oliver lost track of his way in the square. Now where should he go? He consulted his letter of introduction: *Follow Cornhill through Dock Square, and bear to the left,* it read. *That is Union Street. Once through the square you may go left or straight on. Either way will take you to Hanover Street.*

Oliver put the letter away and hurried across the square. He found Hanover Street exactly as described. Houses on both sides of the avenue were handsome brick buildings with white-edged windows and lofty chimney pots. Oliver asked a passing freedman which house was Dr. Church's. It was in mid-block, on the south side. On the hitching post by the curb was a brass cross entwined with serpents. Oliver recognized the caduceus, the ancient symbol of the healing art.

He walked slowly up the brick path and thumped the heavy door knocker. Hardly had he let go of the painted iron ring than the door opened partway. A slave woman, about twice Oliver's age, stood in the gap. Her homespun dress was neatly starched, and a crisp white cap was pinned to her hair.

"Who are you?"

"My name is Oliver Carter. I am here to see Dr. Church."

She frowned. "The doctor don't see sick people here. This is his house."

From behind the door a female voice loudly questioned, "Lily! Who are you talking to? How many times do I have to tell you not to stand in the door when visitors call?"

The door swung wide. A tall woman with a pale powdered face appeared in the dark opening. Her dark brown hair was elaborately curled. She was dressed in a fine blue silk gown. She had the look of a lady, but her manner was arch and angry.

She pushed the slave aside. "Back to the scullery," she said. With a bob of her head, Lily disappeared into the house.

"I am Mrs. Church. Who are you, young man?" the lady asked coldly.

Oliver repeated his name and offered his letter of introduction. "My husband is not at home," said Mrs. Church. "Each day at this time, save Sunday, he is at his dispensary."

"Thank you, ma'am. Where might that be?"

"Cross Street. Good day." With that she shut the door firmly in his face.

The morning was halfway gone to noon. Hunger gnawed at his belly. Oliver had not eaten since yesterday. He had counted on Dr. Church's hospitality. But his wife showed no sign of that.

Better to try the back door for a handout. He circled around to the alley that separated the Churches' house from its neighbor. It was a dank, narrow lane, smothered in moss. He peeked around the back corner of the house. Nothing unusual about the backyard: a patch of green grass, a well, a log cookhouse, an outhouse, and a clothesline bowed under the weight of much snowy linen. As Oliver was taking it all in, Lily came out the back door, carrying a basket of dirty laundry. Though he ducked back, she saw him.

"What are you doing there?" she said, not very loudly.

Oliver stepped into the open. "I was hoping to get something to eat."

Lily laughed. "And the missus didn't offer you any?"

She descended the stone steps and headed for the cookhouse. At the door she said, "Well, come on, I ain't passing out fancy invitations."

Oliver darted across the yard. He glanced back at the house, expecting to see Mrs. Church's severe face glaring at him. The windows were vacant.

It was hot in the cookhouse. It was little more than a large fireplace with walls and a roof around it. A large cauldron sat steaming by the fire. Lily shook out the family linen and lowered each piece into the hot water.

"Look on the table," she advised. "There's parts of breakfast left."

Oliver bit into a hard roll, found some hoop cheese and a

blue china bowl with a few smoked herrings in it. An earthenware pitcher stood nearby. He sniffed it. Buttermilk.

"So," he mumbled through a mouthful of bread. "What's Dr. Church like?"

Lily set the basket down. "He's a good master, I s'pose. He don't beat me or the children." She whittled off thick slices of brown soap from a brick-sized piece and added them to the cauldron. "A good doctor, too. He cured my ague this past winter, and a flux I had last spring."

"He must be rich."

"Richer than you and me. Dresses fine, and he owns two nice houses."

Oliver ate some cheese—good English cheddar. He asked Lily about Mrs. Church.

Lily's forehead furrowed. She said, "They say people marry the opposites of what they are." She stabbed the soap knife into the cake, burying the blade several inches. "Take what I say about the doctor and turn it around, there you got the missus." She dusted her hands on her spotless apron. "You better get on now. If the missus finds out you been here, I'll catch the devil for it."

Oliver slid to his feet. "Sorry," he said, wiping his mouth with his hands. "I don't mean to cause trouble."

"Trouble's like hair. Everybody's got it, some more than others."

Before he left, Oliver got directions to Cross Street. Lily told him to follow Hanover Street past Union, over the bridge on Mill Creek. Hanover became Middle Street in old Boston. Cross Street was the first intersection on Middle.

Nearing his destination, he could smell the waterfront strongly, coming from Mill Pond on his left. Houses lining Middle Street were unmistakably warped by wind and salt air. Most of them were homes of ships' officers—not captains, who lived in grander places farther south, or common seamen, who kept to the dingier row houses on the waterfront. Cross Street was home to navigators and first mates, boatswains and ships' clerks.

In the center of the block, was a narrow brick building, three stories high with an attic on top. Hanging from a post in front of the house was a giant mortar and pestle sign. This was the dispensary of Dr. Benjamin Church.

Most doctors saw patients in a consulting room in their home, or traveled to where they were needed. Dr. Church had enough money to own his pharmacy. It was a handy spot to see patients as well.

In line at the door, he saw two sailors in canvas pants and short jackets, a mother with a coughing boy about ten, and a broad-shouldered fellow Oliver took to be a stevedore. Unpacking ships all day built powerful muscles. Weaving through them, Oliver entered the dispensary. Dr. Church, in powdered white wig and pale blue waistcoat, was seated in a ladder-back chair, gazing down the throat of a teenage girl. The doctor looked about forty years old, with a high forehead, pale complexion, and deeply set eyes. His coat was off and his sleeves rolled back, revealing slender arms as pale as his face.

"Take your place in line, young man. I will get to you soon enough."

"I'm not sick," Oliver explained. "My name is Oliver Carter. I'm a journeyman apothecary from New York. Aren't you expecting me, sir?"

"You're Carter? Welcome, welcome. Take a seat, will you, while I finish this examination." He spoke with a great deal of polished authority, the kind of voice that made people want to do what he said.

Oliver found a chair by the front window and sat down, setting his bundle on the floor between his feet.

"Now, Mary Anne, I've warned you about sleeping with the windows open," the doctor said good-naturedly. "You've got the croup again. I can help you, but you'll keep getting sick as long as you persist in sleeping in drafty rooms."

"Yeth, doctor," the girl said, her jaw stretched wide.

Dr. Church made a few notations in his case book. "Carter," he said without looking up. "What would you prescribe for croup?"

Croup was a sore throat with a cough. Oliver answered, "Honey, lemon, and oil of cayenne, mixed two for one with spirits."

"In what dose?"

"One spoonful, three times a day, before breakfast, before lunch, and before bed."

Dr. Church nodded emphatically. "Very good. Mary Anne, you shall have as Carter prescribes." The girl, Oliver's age and a servant by her dress, glanced over her shoulder at him. Her mouth was still agape.

"Close your mouth, child." She obeyed with a loud snap.

Dr. Church wrote out the prescription in a precise hand and gave it to the girl. He told her to pass on through to the back of the dispensary, where it would be filled. Mary Anne curtsied and put two coins in the bowl by the doctor's hand.

Before she went, Dr. Church cleared his throat, saying, "It's twelve pence, Mary Anne."

The girl wrung her hands and stammered, "My mistress only gave me ten, sir."

"So I see. Your mistress always tries to ignore my rates, which I changed more than a year ago." Seeing the girl trembling, he added, "Go on with you. I shall bill your lady for the balance. But tell her to mind my rates in the future."

"Yes, Dr. Church."

She vanished with a hiss of starched linen. The next patient, the husky stevedore, advanced from the door. Dr. Church halted him with a word.

"A moment, please." Dr. Church dipped a quill in his inkwell and made a few more notes in his casebook.

"Carter," he said, smiling. His teeth were dark and rather crooked, spoiling an otherwise handsome face. "Have you a letter for me?"

Oliver presented his introduction. The doctor broke the

seal and opened the letter. He read silently, his hooded eyes moving across the page.

"Dr. Whitmore speaks well of you," he said. "He says you roll the tightest pills he's seen in thirty year's practice." Oliver modestly said nothing. "You're honest, you have a good memory, and never need to be told the same order twice."

He looked up from the letter. "That's good enough for me. You're hired."

Oliver rose to his feet.

"Thank you, sir! I shall do my best, sir."

The doctor tapped Whitmore's letter to his lips as he thought. "You shall have five shillings a week." That was a pound a month, decent wages but not fabulous. "You may board here in the dispensary. The top floor room has a bed and chamber pot. You will not only compound my medicines, you will sweep out the building twice a day, keep an inventory of my drugs, and collect payments according to the schedule I provide. How does that sound?"

It was fair, and Oliver said so. He expected to shake the doctor's hand to seal the bargain, but Dr. Church kept his hands to himself.

"Well, don't just stand there," the doctor said with a laugh. "Go and fill Mary Anne's prescription."

Honey, lemon, and oil of cayenne, two for one in spirits (rum, naturally, in Boston). *A.C. t.i.d.*, the doctor had written. The Latin initials stood for *ante cibum* (before meals) and *ter in die*, three times a day.

Oliver had a new job and a new home.

chapter two

Services Rendered

As Oliver swept the consulting room before closing, two men burst through the open doorway. One had his arm around the other, holding him up. The supported man had a dark blanket around his shoulders. His face was white with pain. As his companion eased him in, he bumped the injured man against the door frame. The draped man hissed an oath through clenched teeth.

"What's this?" said Dr. Church. He had been preparing to leave for the evening.

"Broken arm, sir," said the man holding up his comrade.

Off came the doctor's elegant coat. Oliver took it and hung it back on its peg. Dr. Church helped the injured man sit down. The doctor turned back the blanket from the man's shoulders, revealing the red coat of a British soldier.

The uninjured man said, "Aye, we're both in His Majesty's service."

"The 64th Regiment has a very good surgeon," the doctor said. "Why don't you return to your barracks and let him treat you?"

"Can't," gritted the soldier with the broken arm.

Dr. Church raised an eyebrow ever so slightly. He called for instruments. Oliver got out the mahogany box the doctor kept his tools in. In one swift motion, Dr. Church slit the man's scarlet sleeve from wrist to shoulder with a thin knife.

"'Ere!" said the other soldier. "Them jackets come out of our pay!"

"So does my fee," Dr. Church replied curtly. "Don't tell me how to doctor, and I won't tell you how to soldier."

A great purple bruise completely encircled the man's upper left arm. Dr. Church examined him with great care. He worked his way down the arm to the soldier's hand. The injured man had more bruises on his forearm. His knuckles were scraped raw.

"How many were you brawling with?" asked the doctor.

"Five," said the white-faced soldier.

"Six," said his comrade. "Damned Yankees. They jumped us and beat us with sticks—"

"Why?"

"Why? Because we're soldiers of the king, that's why!"

Dr. Church slowly unbent the man's broken arm. He cursed quite a bit, using words Oliver had never heard before.

"Where did this take place?" When the soldiers didn't answer, Dr. Church said, "What tavern were you in?"

25

"The Green Dragon."

The doctor looked up from his work, plainly startled. "You picked a poor place to drink. The Green Dragon is practically the headquarters of the Sons of Liberty. Your regiment has been in Boston a long time. Did no one tell you?"

Sheepishly, neither man answered. Dr. Church ordered the soldier in civilian clothes to stand behind his friend and clasp his arms around the injured man's chest.

He beckoned Oliver. "Sit on his legs, Carter." The doctor needed his patient immobilized so he could set the fracture.

The soldier and the young apothecary took their places. Dr. Church stepped back. In the failing light a slight sheen of sweat stood out on his high forehead. Almost casually he took hold of the soldier's wrist with both hands. Without any warning he gave the broken limb a sudden, hard jerk.

The Englishman howled in pain. His comrade strained hard to hold him, shouting "Easy, Jack, be easy!" in his friend's ear.

Dr. Church examined him again. From a small vial he poured a thin stream of olive oil over the site of the break. He spread this around with his fingers, then wrapped the broken arm firmly with a roll of cotton bandage. Taking two hardwood splints, Dr. Church cut them to length and lashed them to the soldier's arm with more bandage.

"Too tight?" he asked when finished. The soldier shook his head. "Can you move your fingers?" With effort he could.

The doctor poured two measures of the cheap brandy he kept on hand for medical purposes. He told the soldiers to drink up. They did. When he quoted his price for setting the arm, they almost choked. Oliver was shocked, too.

"All we got is three shillings," said the healthy man. Dr. Church pocketed the coins, but he advised the men to come up with the rest quickly, or he would report the incident to their company sergeant. The soldiers protested.

"You come to town off duty, visit a known hostile tavern, and get involved in a brawl. Why shouldn't I report you?" Dr. Church replied.

"We didn't mean any harm. It's bloody boring on that island—"

"Robert Moore is your sergeant, isn't he? Roman nose, chin with a deep cleft in it?"

That silenced them. After fitting the injured soldier with a sling, Dr. Church showed them the door. Draped in his blanket, the injured redcoat with his companion disappeared down the darkened street, leaning hard on each other.

Dr. Church shut the dispensary door. "What a day!" he declared. "I promise Carter, they aren't all like this."

Oliver tidied up, putting away the instruments and medicines. He was about to make his way upstairs to his room when Dr. Church said, "You'll be wanting this, I think."

He shook his closed hand and coins clinked. "You're down to your last farthing, aren't you?" Oliver admitted he was completely broke. "Take this then," said the doctor. "Get yourself some roast beef and a mug of ale." He looked down at Oliver's feet. "And a new pair of shoes."

Dr. Church slipped the coins into Oliver's upturned hand. He knew without looking it was a week's pay in advance. He thanked the doctor heartily.

A carriage rattled up outside. Dr. Church set his hat on his head and gave it a light tap to set it in place.

"We're closed tomorrow, it being Sunday," he reminded Oliver. "I may have home visits. If I need any compounding I'll send my coachman, Ezekiel Brown, with the necessary prescriptions."

Dr. Church walked out with short, precise steps. With his hat in place, he was every inch a gentleman.

In the street, Oliver worked up the nerve to ask, "Why did you charge those men so much to set a broken arm?"

"They are buying my silence, lad, in addition to my art. They would be flogged for brawling if they reported to the regimental surgeon. Damned fools." He clucked his tongue in disgust. "Soldiers may not be quartered in Boston, but they still spend their pay here. Did they think they could go into the favored tavern of the Sons of Liberty—in uniform, no less— and not pay a price?"

"Must be a rough place," Oliver said.

"Heaven is unfriendly if the Devil visits." Dr. Church laughed lightly, swinging his gold-headed cane. "And hell is a hard place for saints, which our friends tonight were not."

Across the street, the carriage stood waiting, drawn by a pair of sleek black horses. It was the doctor's, driven by his man Ezekiel Brown.

"Good evening, Brown," Dr. Church called. "How fares Mrs. Church?"

Brown was a tall, bony man who seemed to be all elbows, knees, and fingers. He shifted uncomfortably on the elevated coach seat.

"Fit to be tied, sir. You have guests for dinner, and the missus won't like it that we're late," he muttered.

"You won't like it if I pack you back to Gloucester without a position," the doctor said sharply. "Bless me, who is your employer, Mrs. Church or myself?"

"Yourself, sir."

Dr. Church drew in a deep breath. "I've told you, Brown. Don't be afraid of Mrs. Church. You have to please me, not my wife."

From his brief encounter with Mrs. Church that morning, Oliver understood Brown's predicament. Mrs. Church may not have had the power to discharge him, but she could make his life miserable if he displeased her.

Dr. Church waited for Brown to get down and hold the coach door for him. It was a small conveyance, seating two side by side, with a fold-down seat for others facing. The body was enameled in glossy black, matching the horse team. It was an expensive rig.

The doctor pulled the door shut. "Good night, Carter," he said genially.

"Good night, sir."

Brown climbed to his box and slapped the reins, causing the horses to leap forward. Dr. Church was thrown back in his seat. He called Brown a rascal and an oaf, among other things. Oliver noted his new employer's easy transition from smiling to sharp-tongued. He'd have to watch his step.

Where Cross Street met Middle Street the coach turned left and disappeared around the corner. Oliver locked the front door of the dispensary with the key Dr. Church had given him and went to find a good meal. Not knowing Boston, he decided to take the doctor's route. By the time he reached Middle Street, Dr. Church's coach was out of sight. He trudged up the hill, looking for tavern signs. One small place he passed was called The Saracen's Beard. He went on another block to Union Street. Before he knew it, he was standing in front of the very establishment Dr. Church had spoken of, the Green Dragon Tavern.

Night had fallen. Lanterns on the steps glowed just enough to highlight the low stoop. The tavern was a brick building two stories tall, with three attic windows peering down from the roof like the hooded eyes of a sea creature. Mounted on a curl of iron over the front door was the dragon of the tavern's name, wing upraised and tongue darting forth.

The door opened. Heat and light shone forth. Two men, merry with drink, emerged laughing.

Seeing the crowd inside, Oliver decided to double back to the less busy Saracen's Beard. There a stout African woman served him beans and rice, washed down with hard cider. He ate until he thought he'd burst. It was the best meal he'd had since leaving New York.

Returning to the dispensary, Oliver climbed to his empty, dusty room and fell gratefully on the straw-filled mattress. His repose was short-lived. An hour after falling asleep, the sound of shattering glass startled Oliver. He rolled quickly to his feet. No other sounds followed the glass breaking. Heartbeat hammering in his ears, he armed himself with a piece of firewood and went downstairs, expecting to confront an intruder.

The shop was empty. One of the diamond-shaped windowpanes had been smashed. On the floor rested a small white object, barely visible in the moonlight.

He picked it up. A stone, wrapped in a scrap of cloth. And something else, something round and hard.

Oliver undid the knot in the rag. A coin fell out. The redcoat with the broken arm had paid his bill sooner than expected.

Sunday morning, Oliver rose early. Devouring cold biscuits he'd brought home from the Saracen's Beard, he set out to find Boston's Church of England, King's Chapel. The old woman at the tavern had said it was located on the corner of School Street and Tremont. Before leaving, Oliver slipped the cloth and coin in his pocket for Dr. Church.

At this hour, the city was alive as much as on a market day. Oliver lost count of the families he saw, prayerbooks clasped in their hands. Fathers led the way, followed by their wives. Close behind walked the children, struggling to be serious in the same streets where they usually ran and played. Shooing them along (at least in the wealthier families) were servants or slaves.

In Hanover Street, Oliver spotted the black carriage drawn up in front of Dr. Church's house. He saw Mrs. Church and two young ladies he took to be the doctor's daughters. They were preparing to enter the coach. Ezekiel Brown stood by the open coach door, a hand extended to help the women board.

Oliver removed his hat and said, "Good morning, ma'am. Is the doctor in?"

She studied him with icy blue eyes. "The doctor does not see patients on Sunday morning."

"I'm the doctor's new apothecary, Oliver Carter."

The younger Church daughter climbed into the coach. The elder, who was close to Oliver's age, watched him keenly until her mother shooed her into the coach.

"Dr. Church is within. Since he cannot trouble himself to attend services, I'm sure he will receive you."

"I'm on my way to service myself," said Oliver. "There is a small matter I have to bring to the doctor's attention."

"What church do you attend?" asked the older daughter, leaning forward to see him through the open door.

"Church of England."

She smiled. "King's Chapel is our church!"

She was cut off by her mother slamming the door.

"Good day," she said. Brown climbed onto the driver's box, took the reins, and drove on.

Oliver knocked on the front door. He expected Lily to answer, but instead a young woman with honey-colored hair drawn back in a bun opened the door. She had the gentlest brown eyes Oliver had ever seen.

"Yes?"

"Oliver Carter to see Dr. Church."

"Moment, please." She had a noticeable accent. Dutch maybe, or German?

He heard the doctor's voice: "Show him in, Hilde." The servant girl stepped back, holding the door for him. Oliver walked in, nodding his thanks.

Hilde showed him into the front sitting room. Dr. Church was sitting on a long settee, sipping tea from a delicate china cup. Wrapped in a long, wine red dressing gown, and he was not wearing his wig. Oliver was startled by his appearance. Only thirty-nine, the good doctor was bald as an egg.

"What brings you out so early?"

He told Dr. Church about the broken window and the coin. Frowning, the doctor asked to see the money. Oliver handed it to him.

"You saw no one?"

"I was in my room upstairs."

"Yes, of course." He closed the coin in his fist. "A man of affairs like myself is bound to have enemies."

"Surely this is the work of those soldiers, the one whose arm you set last evening?"

Dr. Church looked up, surprised. "You may be right. At any rate, thank you for bringing this to my attention."

Sensing the meeting was over, Oliver said good-bye. Dr. Church resumed reading the papers he had cast aside. He rang for more tea. Lily appeared with a tray, while Hilde stood in the doorway with Oliver's hat.

He went to the door. Taking his hat he said in a low voice, "Is the doctor ill?"

Hilde replied, "Why, no."

"Why didn't he go to church with his family?"

She struggled to find the right words. "Dr. Church, he is, *wass bedeute, ein Philosoph*—"

"A philosopher?"

"Yes. He is not a churchly man."

He smiled. "Well, good-bye and thank you."

She shut the door behind him. Oliver found himself wishing she hadn't.

The bells were ringing when Oliver reached King's Chapel. It was an imposing stone building, with a squat, square steeple and columned porch. He joined the last surge of worshipers going in. Once inside, he discovered why the church was so full—at least half the congregation were redcoat soldiers or officers. The ferries from Castle Island must have been busy all morning bringing soldiers across the harbor for church. Near the altar sat the highest ranks, men with gold epaulets and neatly powdered wigs. Lesser ranks sat in the middle, and the rank and file in the very back. Mixed in with the officers were well-to-do Bostonians, including Mrs. Church and her daughters.

The vicar was a well-spoken man, learned and grave. His message about a Christian's duty to obey God (and God's appointed) cannot have failed to please those seated under the vicar's eye.

When the service finished, the congregation rose and the vicar led them out, beginning with the officers, royal officials, and wealthy Bostonians. Mrs. Church went out on the arm of a splendidly dressed officer. Two serving women in the pew behind Oliver gossiped that the doctor's wife enjoyed the company of General Haldimand, temporary commander of His Majesty's forces in America. The overall commander, General Thomas Gage, was in England.

Oliver emerged from church feeling restless. Sunday afternoon was his own time, but what to do with it? Two days in Boston, and Oliver had yet to discover what diversions the city had to offer.

chapter three

Under the Liberty Tree

Boston on Sunday afternoon proved to be a very quiet town. From a passing workman, Oliver learned that good fishing could be had at Windmill Point, on the southeast side of town. With Dr. Church's coins in his pocket, the sun shining, and the early heat of summer in the air, Oliver decided to try his hand at fishing. For a few pennies he could buy a rod and some bait, and maybe catch enough fish to keep his frying pan full for a few days.

Passing through town he saw plenty of people coming from church, or on their way to visit friends or family for Sunday dinner. Many soldiers were about, strolling in threes and fours down the wider streets, eyeing local girls and voicing their opinions too loudly. The farther south Oliver went, the quieter the streets became. Very soon the streets were empty, save for scrounging dogs and an occasional passing carriage.

When he reached the corner of Winter Street, he heard an ominous sound. It was a drum, beating a steady tempo. The only reason Oliver could think of a drum on a quiet Sunday afternoon was to raise an alarm. He saw no smoke or fire rising from the rooftops. Who was beating the drum, and why?

He had arrived at an irregular square formed by the meeting of four streets. The sign at his back read Essex Street. Across the square, a crowd had gathered in the yard of a large gabled house. A head-high wall surrounded the yard but the gate was open, allowing the crowd to spill out into the street. A grand elm tree towered over everything, well budded out by the warm spell. From everything he had heard, Oliver realized he was looking at the famous Liberty Tree.

On this spot, eight years ago, resistance to the Stamp Act blossomed. Parliament in England imposed the hated stamp tax on all manner of official and private documents—from deeds to common newspapers—as a way of raising revenue from the colonies. Americans from New Hampshire to Georgia exploded in anger. Pay taxes? When the colonies had no representatives in Parliament to speak for them? That was tyranny!

There were speeches and meetings held under the Liberty Tree every day. English goods were boycotted. Stamp holders and tax collectors were chased out of town. The uproar grew so great that Parliament backed down and repealed the Stamp Act in 1766. Here, at the Liberty Tree, was where the infamous act was brought low.

Oliver edged closer, curious as to what new outrage had drawn the people of Boston to the tree. There were already a few hundred in the crowd: mechanics in working clothes, gentlemen in silk and satin, idlers, freedmen, and ordinary folk still dressed for church. Oliver could hear someone speaking in a loud voice, but he could not make out the words. Neither could those around him, and a shout went up for the speaker to come out from behind the wall so all could hear.

Instead, six husky men boosted the speaker atop the wall ringing the yard. With strong, callused hands bracing the backs of his calves, the man stood erect.

"Friends! Fellow *Americans*," he said with added emphasis, "The time is not far off when Parliament will find some new duty to impose on us! Mark it well! A new tax is coming! And why, you ask? The noble gentlemen of Parliament want us to believe we are paying our share of the late war against the French. Don't believe it, friends! Our men fought the Indians and French. Our men died by hatchet and fire—is it not so? Our towns raised corn and cattle for the army. Our ships transported the king's troops to Canada. We *paid* for our war in blood! Why should we pay for it again with our hard-won gold?"

The speaker paused to gulp from a wooden tankard held up to him on a forked stick. As he quenched his thirst, many in the crowd echoed his sentiments. A few listeners raised objections. They were swiftly shouted down.

"Americans! I will tell you why Parliament so desires our money. If we do not fill their coffers with our coin, they will have to squeeze the people of England for it. They need gold to pay the debts piled up fighting the French, and the bankers will have their pound of flesh! The noble lords and gentlemen of Parliament dare not tax their own people too far—they must win their votes! Why should they tax them, when they have hardworking Americans to bleed?"

Skeptics in the crowd booed and hissed. "Lies! Slander!" they called.

Others shouted, "God save the king!"

"God save the king?" the speaker retorted. "If only the king would save us! His ministers plot to put us into the poorhouse! Our highly esteemed governor, the Honorable Mr. Hutchinson, stands ready to pick our pockets and plunder our accounts to please his masters in London. No new taxes, I say! When they come—and they will—mark these words I say to you: No taxation without representation! No gold for parliamentary palaces or bankers' banquets!"

The assembly answered with enthusiasm. There were a few in the crowd who called the speaker a traitor, which earned them fists from surrounding liberty men. The speaker laughed and urged the crowd to show Parliament's loyal subjects how Americans felt about greedy tax collectors masquerading as honest men.

The crowd surged toward the scuffling. Oliver tried to back out of the way. He bumped into someone large and solid standing behind him.

Oliver said, "Beg pardon," glancing over his shoulder to see whose foot he'd stepped on.

He was a broad man, well made, dressed in somber brown broadcloth. His face was fleshy but regular, and his eyes spoke of much intelligence and good humor.

"Don't you like Brother William's message?" asked the man. His voice matched his expression, strong but contained.

"Brother William?"

"Mr. William Molineux." He held up a hand to the speaker, who was watching the fistfights with evident satisfaction.

"Mr. Molineux knows how to stir folks up," said Oliver politely.

The man laughed heartily. "I'll tell him you said that!"

A well-dressed man, his stock askew and one sleeve of his fine blue silk coat torn off, reeled past. Blood was running from his nose, and his lower lip looked like a sausage ready for the frying pan. He stumbled away from Oliver and the man in brown. His eyes were wide with fright. Hot on his heels came four burly workmen.

He'll need arnica for his bruises tonight, thought Oliver.

"That's the thing about liberty," said the man, watching the battered gentleman flee down Essex Street, hotly pursued. "It must be fought for."

Oliver saw again in his mind the Royal Navy schooner ablaze, flames climbing the rigging and leaping from the masthead. Fighting for liberty was dangerous business, not like a foppish clerk being roughed up by four toughs. Not wishing to share his past with a stranger, Oliver simply nodded. The man in brown smiled, and he walked away through the gate into the courtyard with the Liberty Tree. His entrance was greeted with hearty cheers.

Molineux got down from the wall. The drum rattled again, and the meeting began to break up, just in time. One of the roughed-up friends of the government must have summoned the town watch. They came down Newbury Street at the double, banging a drum of their own. They were men of Boston, too, and some might have been liberty men, but brawling on the Sabbath was not to be tolerated.

People poured out of the garden gate. They didn't run, nor did they linger too long under the Liberty Tree. One of the last ones out was William Molineux. Oliver noticed he was red faced even when he wasn't haranguing a mob. With him was the sturdy fellow in brown. The latter spotted Carter and touched a hand to his head in passing salute.

The watchmen's drum grew louder and louder. Long in the habit of avoiding official scrutiny, Oliver darted down Essex Street. Once out of the way, he looked back in time to see the last man leave the shade of the Liberty Tree. To his surprise, he knew the man—Ezekiel Brown, Dr. Church's coachman. Brown did not run away like the others. He slipped along the garden wall with unexpected grace, heading straight into the arms (and cudgels) of the watch. Oliver didn't wait to see more. He ran down the sunny lane until the drumbeat had faded behind him.

By coincidence he was near his original destination, Windmill Point. At the bottom of Essex Street he bought a pole, line, and bait from an old sailor for threepence.

Oliver passed a pleasant afternoon. He caught three fish. He only kept one, a steel-colored mackerel as long as his forearm. The other two he sold to the pier master for bait.

Shadows were long when he walked home along the waterfront. Though it was Sunday, there was work aplenty as cargoes from England and the Caribbean were brought ashore to waiting warehouses. Outgoing trade was piled on the docks, ready to be loaded when the ships' holds were empty. It was Sunday, but the tide observed no Sabbath.

Oliver had intended to go straight to the dispensary. He was pink from the sun and chapped by sea breezes, his shoes held together only by God's grace. He had a willow pole and a fish in his hands. Not exactly in a fit state for a social call, he kept thinking about Dr. Church's servant girl, and his thought diverted him to Hanover Street.

There was a lighted lantern out front of the Churches' house. Oliver imagined the lantern was lit because the Church family was out. Encouraged by his deduction, Oliver hurried down the lane to the back door.

Before he reached the rear steps he knew he had miscalculated. A voice was screaming inside the house. Oliver froze. He was about to retreat when the door opened. Lily backed out, holding a candle. She sensed Oliver's presence and flinched.

"Go 'way!" Lily whispered. "The missus is in a rage!"

One of Oliver's feet dropped backward on the step. "What's Dr. Church done?"

"It's not the doctor she's chastisin'. It's the maid!"

He had no business interfering between a servant and her mistress. The very least that could happen was he would lose his valuable new position. Leave now, that was Oliver's resolution. He meant to, but before he could slip away he heard another, uglier sound—the impact of fist on flesh.

He thrust his pole and fish on Lily, then pushed past her into the house. His shoes thumped on the carpet. Cold resolve overcame any fear he had about retribution.

Hilde cowered in the space below the stairs, hands crossed in front of her face. Mrs. Church had her by the collar. As Oliver advanced, she hit the girl again on the ear.

"Stupid, stupid wench!" the doctor's wife railed. "Those curtains are Flanders lace! Do you know how much they cost? Do you?" Her hand went up for another blow.

It never landed. To her astonishment, Mrs. Church found her wrist held fast. When she saw who had stopped her, her eyes widened with fury.

"Release me!" she gasped. "Insolent boy, how dare you touch me!"

"Let her go," Oliver said quietly. He dared not speak up for fear his voice would break.

Mrs. Church struggled in his grasp. She let go of Hilde's collar, and for a moment, Oliver thought she would strike him, but his expression convinced her not to. Hilde sagged to her knees, trembling. Seeing she was free, Oliver released Mrs. Church's arm.

"You are finished," she said hoarsely. "When the doctor finds out what you've done—"

The front doorknob rattled. "There he is now!" Oliver squared his shoulders, ready to meet his fate.

The door swung in, revealing the doctor. Brown, the coachman behind him, held a stout walking stick. Dr. Church took in the scene. Spying his young daughters on the landing above, he sharply ordered them to bed. Whispering excitedly, they scurried upstairs.

"What is this, Hannah?" Dr. Church demanded.

Mrs. Church drew away from Hilde and Oliver. "This boy laid hands on me!"

"Really? Now why would he do that?"

"Sir, if I may speak?" Oliver began, but Mrs. Church screamed him into silence.

Dr. Church took his wife by the elbow and said severely, "Have you lost your senses? Calm yourself at once!"

To the coachman he said, "That will be all, Brown." With a respectful nod, Ezekiel withdrew, shutting the door.

"Do you know the whole street heard your screeching?" the doctor said. "Old Mrs. Whitcomb met me at the curb. She thought you must be fending off a pack of brigands. That's why I had Brown come in with me."

He let her go. Mrs. Church sagged into a side chair, glaring at Oliver.

He ignored her. Kneeling beside Hilde, he saw blood on her starched white apron. Her nose was bleeding. A trickle of crimson ran out of her ear.

"Doctor," he said. "Her eardrum is broken."

Dr. Church examined Hilde. Bruises were plain on her face and arms. He gave the girl a silk handkerchief from his pocket to wipe her nose.

"You burst her eardrum," he told his wife. "Why?"

"The clumsy wench scorched my new lace draperies while ironing them." Mrs. Church gave Hilde a poisonous look. "Stupid girl doesn't understand English!"

"I've never had any trouble communicating with her." The doctor held Hilde's hand and helped her to her feet. "Go to your room, girl. I will tend to you shortly."

Hilde slipped by Oliver without meeting his eyes. While the situation was too public for any sort of a thank-you, he had at least hoped for a grateful glance.

"What about him?" Mrs. Church said, her voice rising. "He raised his hand to me!"

45

"Did he strike you?" She admitted he had not. The doctor inspected his wife's slender wrist. It was red and chafed, but otherwise unhurt.

"In my medical opinion you will survive." Mrs. Church opened her mouth to protest, but the doctor said, "You may go to your room now, too."

She rose with a rustle of silk.

"Will you do nothing to defend my honor?"

"Carter will await my displeasure on the morrow," Dr. Church said. "Good night, Carter."

With a heavy heart, Oliver retraced his steps to the back door. Lily was there, listening in the shadows. As he passed, she returned his pole and fish, and shut the door behind him.

chapter four

Oliver's Patient

After a restless night, Oliver got up with the sun. He packed his few belongings and put the bundle by the door.

Dr. Church arrived at nine, humming a song and twirling his cane. Oliver opened the door for him. Surveying the consulting room, the doctor expressed surprise things were not set up to receive the day's patients.

Oliver hurried to get jars of often-used medicines, laid the doctor's casebook on the table, and swept off the front step. Dr. Church sat at his table leafing through a newspaper he'd brought with him, the *Boston Gazette*.

He eyed the broken windowpane. Oliver asked if he should cover it with a piece of paper.

"No, it's a warm day," the doctor said. "Run to Clarke's Square to the glazier and have him fix it."

Oliver returned with a man to mend the window and found three patients waiting. So far, Dr. Church had said nothing about the incident with his wife. Puzzled, Oliver went to the back room to prepare any required medication.

More patients arrived: a farmer with boils, a tradesman's wife with a fever, a fisherman with an arm slashed by a rusty hook. This last fellow was a tough old salt. He sat perfectly still, puffing his stinking pipe as Dr. Church put twenty-nine stitches in his wound.

The sun was high in the street when the doctor closed the door for lunch. Oliver was in the back room cleaning a mortar when he heard him call.

"I'm away for luncheon, Carter," he said, consulting a thick pocket watch. "I shall be back by one o' clock."

Sunlight slanting in from the street cast shadows on the wall of the consulting room. Painted lines indicated the hours by the position of the shadows.

"Sir!" Oliver said as Dr. Church turned to go. "About last night—"

"Yes?"

"Am I dismissed?"

Dr. Church slipped his watch into his waistcoat pocket. "Have I said so?"

Oliver didn't know what to say. He had laid hands on his employer's wife and interfered with domestic affairs. How could he not be dismissed?

"Look here, Carter, I'm due at the Green Dragon. We shall discuss last night's little drama later, eh?"

He went out. Oliver sat down at his workbench. For

whatever reason, mercy and Dr. Church had smiled on him. As the truth dawned, he resumed cleaning the big mortar, whistling as he scraped the granite bowl. He was not going to lose his job. Oliver had no idea why Dr. Church extended this great favor to him, but he could not complain.

The shadow on the front wall crept to the one mark. The doctor did not return. Slowly the dark line advanced onto the two. Patients rattled the door, wanting in. Oliver had to plead for their patience, but as the two o' clock hour passed, the sick and injured sought treatment elsewhere.

It was nearly three when Oliver heard a quiet knock at the door. He set aside the sulfur flowers he had sifted and went to see who was there. The good day suddenly got better. Hilde stood outside. She had a bandage rolled around her head. It held a pad of cotton on her injured ear.

"Come in," he said. Without a word she crossed the threshold. Hilde sat down in the consulting chair.

"Dr. Church isn't here."

She looked a little distressed. "No? I was told to come at this hour."

"He should be back at any time." Oliver was actually rather worried. Dr. Church had been away so long Oliver wondered if something might be wrong. Even so, he was happy to have this moment with Hilde. He sat down in the doctor's chair facing her.

"How is your ear?"

"Hurting. It is like someone has filled my head with candle wax. I can hear nothing on that side."

"Perhaps the dressing needs changing." Oliver pulled out the pin holding the bandage in place and carefully unrolled it. Hilde sat perfectly still, eyes downcast. When the last layer of cloth came away, the pad came with it. It was spotted with dried blood.

"It wants cleaning." He wrapped a piece of clean cotton around the tip of Dr. Church's forceps. With sweet oil and a little spirits of wine he gently sponged away the dried blood.

"Did that hurt?"

She shook her head.

"Why don't you speak then?"

"Speaking gets me in trouble. Speaking English, I mean."

She explained how Mrs. Church had flown into a rage. "Many times she screams at me for not ironing the curtains with sharp enough creases. Four times that day she raised her voice on me. When I burned the lace trying to please her she went, how is it said? Raving mad."

"Has she ever hit you before?"

Hilde nodded. "Some slappings and hair pulling. Also Lily, the housekeeper, is getting slaps. But never a beating with fists. I think the missus is very angry at more than me."

He prompted her to go on, but Hilde would not say any more on the subject. They talked about her. Oliver learned she was fifteen and from Swabia in southern Germany. She had come to America with her parents, but they died, one after the other, from consumption. Destitute, Hilde had indentured herself as a servant. Dr. Church was her first employer.

Oliver said, "I am an orphan, too." His family had died of smallpox in western Pennsylvania during the war with the French. Oliver survived because he'd walked to a neighbor's farm even though he was roasting with fever. The neighbor nursed Oliver back to health.

A heavily laden wagon rolled past the dispensary, rattling the windows.

"I want to thank you," Hilde said slowly. "Coming to my help cannot have been easy."

"I could not stand by and see anyone beaten."

"But yourself—you no longer work for *Herr Arzt*?"

Oliver smiled. "He hasn't dismissed me yet."

She looked doubtful. Though he couldn't explain why, Oliver assured Hilde he was still Dr. Church's apothecary.

"It's simple, my boy. A fellow who rolls pills as hard as yours has a talent not soon given up."

Dr. Church stood in the open doorway, smiling broadly at the two young people. He seemed very pleased about something at that moment.

"Stealing my patients, are you Carter?" he said. The oil, alcohol, and soiled bandage lay on the table.

"Begging your pardon, sir." Oliver stood up and began clearing things away.

Dr. Church hung up his hat and cane. Taking Hilde's chin in his hand, he turned her head so he could see her injured ear.

"It will heal," he assured her. "Our errant Daphne shall hear again." Something in his manner had a mocking quality Oliver didn't like.

Embarrassed, Hilde begged permission to leave. Dr. Church shrugged. Oliver poured up a measure of oil in a small vial and gave it to Hilde with a wad of clean cloth as a bandage. She fled, running up Cross Street.

Oliver watched her from the front window. "Sir, what's an 'errant Daphne?'"

The doctor laughed. "Daphne was a nymph in ancient Greek legend. Pursued by the god Apollo, whom she did not like, she asked her river-god father to save her from Apollo's advances. He turned her into a laurel tree. In honor of his unrequited love, Apollo plucked some leafy twigs and wove the first laurel crown."

His explanation did not help Oliver much. If Hilde was Daphne, who was Apollo?

He told the doctor about his patients leaving. Dr. Church did not seem concerned. "There are always sick people in Boston," he said lightly. "And plenty of damaged folk, too."

It was nearly four o'clock. Word must have gotten around that Dr. Church was out, for no one else showed up at the dispensary seeking treatment. The doctor passed the time writing letters. At one point, Oliver emerged from the back room to find Dr. Church writing with such fervor it seemed he would pierce the paper with his quill.

"What do you want, Carter?" said the doctor. He casually covered his unfinished letter with his left hand.

"The medicinal brandy is almost gone."

"We can't have that." Dr. Church tossed him a large coin. Oliver caught it. It was a gold sovereign.

"That's more than enough for brandy," he said. "Bring me the change tomorrow."

Before the doctor left for the day, Oliver managed to force out some words he dreaded.

"Doctor, please tell me. Why are you forgiving me for stopping Hilde's beating?"

Dr. Church set his elegant gray hat on his head and adjusted the angle just so. The light glinted on the gilded head of his cane.

"No one knows my wife's temper better than I. Mrs. Church has always had a heavy hand with the servants. I'm glad someone stood up to her," he said.

To Oliver this did not ring true. Why allow a young journeyman such liberty? Sensing his skepticism, Dr. Church added, "Mrs. Church went too far. A slap is one thing, but boxing a young girl's ears is quite another. Had I been home, I would have stopped her myself."

Oliver closed the heavy casebook and tucked it under his arm. "What will Mrs. Church do when she finds out I am not discharged?"

"Scream, I expect. Not to worry, my boy. When she does that, I go. The surest way to baffle an angry woman is not to be present."

Chuckling, he departed. It was too early for Brown and the carriage, so Dr. Church strolled off in the warm afternoon, swinging his slender walking stick.

When the dispensary was ready for the next day, Oliver set out to replenish the supply of brandy. With the doctor's coin weighting down his pocket, he left to find a tavern. There were many closer to the waterfront, but he had an idea where to go. Where Union Street crossed his path he bore right and soon stood before the famous Green Dragon. Oliver pushed the door open, removing his hat when he entered.

It was early for supper, so the room was not full. When Oliver came in, talk died. It felt like half the patrons in the room stared at him, while the other half averted their faces so as not to be recognized. The effect was so unnerving Oliver started to leave.

A genial, red-faced man in a leather apron stood by the kitchen door. Sizing up the newcomer he boomed, "Welcome to the Green Dragon. Take your ease anywhere you like!"

Oliver made his way past tables and benches to the back of the room. Another man, gray hair curled in a tight queue, stood behind a Dutch door, polishing pewter tankards. Taking him for the publican, Oliver asked if he could buy some brandy.

"Surely," said the man, setting aside his work. "France or England?"

Since it was for medicinal purposes, it didn't have to be very fine.

"Whatever is cheapest." Oliver bought a quart of English brandy in a stoneware jug.

He paid for the spirits and made for the door. Passing the kitchen door again, he saw a magnificent beef haunch on a spit, turning before an enormous fireplace. A sweating man with a black eye patch basted the beef with a copper dipper. Kettles bubbled and steamed on the hearth. Loaves of newly baked bread were stacked like cordwood on the cook's table. Maybe he would stay for supper. . . .

Oliver sat down at the end of a long table. Three men perched at the opposite end, nursed mugs of brown beer. They watched as Oliver tucked into a platter of beef, onions, and potatoes. When he next looked up from his meal, the men had gone.

The front door opened, and four men came in. There was a general shout of greeting from the patrons. Leading the group was a middle-aged man, short, fleshy, with a long face and hard eyes. Oliver recognized the next man. He was the broad-shouldered man who had taken such an interest in Oliver's presence at the Liberty Tree. He spotted the young apothecary and gave him a friendly nod in greeting.

Leaning on the sturdy man's arm was a portly man clad in black. He wore an old-fashioned white wig. His pale face was swollen, and his neck lined with purplish veins. Unsteady on his feet, he grunted and gasped as he walked. He was a very sick man. The rotund man was greeted on all sides with great respect. Patrons from all walks of life rose when he approached. The fellow with the eye patch, now clearing tables, hailed him as 'Mr. Otis.'

"How's the roast tonight, Peter?" he rasped.

"Rare as Connecticut clay, sir."

The fourth man trailed the others, but he was no less noteworthy. He was a pleasant-looking man, with an intelligent, sensitive face, well dressed in black with a white silk waistcoat. While the others passed by, he stopped at Oliver's table.

"Well now," he said. "Here's a face I don't know."

"I don't know him either, Dr. Warren," said the barkeep. "Never seen him before."

"A Tory informer?" said Dr. Warren, eyeing him with cool deliberation.

Everyone turned to look at Oliver. He felt small under so much scrutiny.

The burly man he'd met at the Liberty Tree came back.

"Leave him be," he said. "He's just a boy."

"Boys can be spies."

Mr. Otis turned ponderously on his tightly swollen legs. "Eh?" he rasped. "Who's a spy?"

"No one, Mr. Otis!" Oliver's defender replied loudly.

Oliver got up, cradling the brandy jug in his arms. "I'll be going," he murmured. Several rough-looking customers blocked his way to the door.

Oliver didn't want a broken arm, like the imprudent redcoat Dr. Church had treated. He wondered how many opponents he could take down with the brandy bottle before the rest got him?

"Let him be."

Oliver's defender put a hand on his shoulder. "Do you think Haldimand or Hutchinson would send an unknown boy into our midst to spy on us?"

"The general and the governor are well informed on our doings," Dr. Warren answered.

"So they are. But they didn't get that way listening to a boy who's never been here before, did they?"

He gave Oliver a little push. "On your way, lad."

Oliver didn't need any more encouragement. He wound his way through the silent men to the tavern door. Dr. Warren followed him, holding the door open for Oliver.

"You have a friend here," he remarked. When Oliver regarded him blankly Dr. Warren said, "Not I." He pointed to the broad-shouldered fellow who'd spoken for Oliver. "You have the honor, young man, of being trusted by Mr. Paul Revere. I hope you deserve it."

chapter five

The Doctor's Way

July 1773

Summer arrived fiercely hot. The heat spoiled food and tainted supplies of drinking water. As a result, digestive ailments swamped Boston's doctors. Oliver developed a touch of the flux, as it was called, which laid him low for a week. Dr. Church, needing his apothecary back at work as soon as possible, sent Hilde to nurse him.

Things had not improved for Hilde. When it became clear Oliver was not going to be punished, Mrs. Church took out her anger on the girl. She did not hit her again, but started deducting sums from Hilde's wages for any mistake. Some weeks went by with Hilde earning nothing at all. No matter how careful Hilde was, Mrs. Church always found reasons to dock her pay. This was doubly hard on Hilde. She could not leave the Churches until she repaid the money they spent buying her indenture.

Hilde turned out to be an excellent nurse. For days Oliver could keep nothing down but clear broth. Hilde sat by his bed, spooning soup into his mouth. She applied cool cloths to his burning forehead. She carried off his chamber pot and took his dirty linen to a washerwoman. When he asked, she agreed to read to him.

"I only read German," she confessed. He didn't mind. She read the Psalms to him in her native language and he would fall asleep, soothed by the sound of her voice.

Oliver got the idea he could teach her to read English. Hilde was willing, but fate intervened before they could get started. Dr. Church abruptly announced that Mrs. Church, his daughters, and the household servants were leaving for their country house in Raynham. There they might escape the flux that affected so many people in Boston. Dr. Church would remain in town.

Hilde told Oliver that Dr. Church's decision was not well received by Mrs. Church. Why should the doctor remain in the city, alone, with no servants to keep house for him? Dr. Church even ordered Ezekiel Brown to Raynham, so his family would have use of the carriage.

Dr. Church's argument (a loud one, Hilde said) was that his work was in Boston. He owed money on the splendid house in Raynham. He had to work hard to pay for the luxuries his family enjoyed.

Propped up in bed, Oliver asked in low voice, "Does the doctor have many debts?"

Eyes darting around, Hilde said, "I fear so. He spends much on his comforts, and the missus will have her fine things, too."

Dr. Church stood firm. His family departed Boston by carriage on June 21. Hilde and Lily followed in a hired wagon piled high with cases of clothing, the family silver, and provisions. Oliver had lost his nurse.

He recovered anyway. On the seventh day of his illness he could stand. On the eighth day he ate solid food again. He tottered downstairs to the dispensary to report his recovery to Dr. Church. Oliver knew the doctor needed him badly. From his window high over Cross Street, Oliver had seen the people lined up in the street outside the dispensary. He was surprised when he reached the bottom of the steps and saw that Dr. Church was not alone with his patients.

Consulting with Dr. Church was the dapper Dr. Warren. Oliver remembered him well from the Green Dragon Tavern. Since their first meeting, he had learned that Warren was a highly regarded physician as well as a leader of the most radical faction of the Sons of Liberty. Rumors around town said that Dr. Warren not only opposed new taxes, he favored independence from Britain altogether.

When Oliver appeared, hollowed-eye from his siege, Dr. Warren said, "What's this, Benjamin? Hiding extra patients upstairs?"

"That's no patient. That's my pill roller, Oliver Carter." Dr. Church beckoned. "Come here, Carter. I'd like you to meet my colleague, Dr. Warren."

"How do you do, sir?" he said. "We have met before, Dr. Warren, at the Green Dragon. You congratulated me on having Mr. Revere's trust."

Dr. Warren didn't bat an eye, but Dr. Church said brusquely, "Have you been frequenting the Green Dragon? Why have I not heard of this before?"

"Calm yourself, Benjamin. The boy hasn't been dabbling in politics. Some of the rougher sort at the tavern took young Carter for an informer. Revere took his part, and that was the end of the matter."

Dr. Church took a deep breath. "If there's no more to it than that, I have no objection."

The two men went back to discussing the sickness sweeping through the city. Supplies of drugs were running low, and only a trickle of new drugs came in from England. Prices were high. They needed more medicine.

"Our friends in Gloucester and Providence have other sources," Dr. Warren said.

"The Dutch?" asked Dr. Church. Warren nodded.

"Smuggling tea is one thing, but I don't like buying my medicines sight unseen," Dr. Church said, frowning.

"I agree, but what can we do? So far the malady has only been debilitating. Unchecked, people will die."

Dr. Church thought for a long moment, then said, "I agree. Who will handle the shipments? Hancock?"

Dr. Warren plainly didn't like hearing the name spoken. "It matters not who lands the medicine, does it? Say how much you will need, and I shall see it is delivered."

Dr. Church made a short computation on a scrap of paper.

"Is this too much?" he said, showing it to Warren. Oliver could not see the figures.

"You have more patients than I, Benjamin!"

"Skill will out, my dear Joseph."

Oliver knew the doctors were talking about opium, smuggled in by Dutch or other foreign traders. Opium was used to make a tincture called laudanum, which was the most effective drug they had against the flux. Dr. Church's supply was so low he had to substitute far weaker drugs like oak gall, which could be found in Massachusetts. Opium was legal to import, but it had to be bought from British sources, who marked up the price greatly. To evade the British monopoly, smuggling was common.

The line of sufferers grew restive. Dr. Warren took his leave, and Dr. Church called for the next patient.

Oliver prepared many a bottle of laudanum that afternoon, diluted with other ingredients to make the supply of opium go further. Weak as he was, Oliver kept mixing and labeling prescriptions past sundown. He was on his last preparation when he heard footsteps approaching. It was Dr. Church, bearing a candle.

"I've bolted the door at last," he said. Flame highlighted his face with eerie shadows. "How are you getting along?"

"Almost done, sir."

Dr. Church watched Oliver work. He said, "You will be the best apothecary in Boston someday." Oliver thanked him. The doctor went on, "But you must be careful in your choice of associates."

Oliver stopped mixing and looked up. "Sir?"

"Dr. Warren is a fine physician with a fine mind, but not all liberty men can make that claim. Some are very dangerous men, my boy. Watch your step."

Oliver said, "Doctor, are you for liberty?"

He smiled. "In all things, Carter."

Oliver took a chance. "I have been a liberty man myself."

Dr. Church raised an eyebrow. "Where was that?" When Oliver did not answer, Dr. Church said slyly, "New York, was it? No wonder you've been so quiet about your beliefs. Shout the wrong slogan on the street in New York, for king or liberty, and you can get your head broken, eh?"

Oliver sealed his last vial of tincture. "Every man of conscience must choose his path."

"How right you are! Tonight I choose to dine with you, Carter. Is your stomach up to it?"

It was. Dr. Church held the candle out so Oliver could see the way. They left the hot, airless dispensary. In the street it was very humid, but at least a breeze was stirring.

"Where shall we go?" asked the doctor, smiling. "The Green Dragon?"

Oliver deferred to his employer.

"I've had enough politics for one day. Come! I know a congenial spot."

They strolled along. Dr. Church swung his cane and spoke expansively about the problems of being a physician in Boston in the Year of Our Lord 1773. Fires, smallpox, the flux every summer, rising costs, the persistent and growing trouble with the government—

He stopped there. "I promised no politics!"

Then, he turned to money. Sighing eloquently, he said no matter how much he made, he never had enough. His wife spent gold like a chicken ate cracked corn. Having only daughters, he had to consider how they would marry, and what their dowries might be.

"Money is like a beautiful woman," he declared. "No matter now much you love her, you always want more."

In King Street, he stopped before a tavern. The sign over the door showed a colt capering in a field of flowers.

"Ah, The Gambols," the doctor said.

It was clear from his reception Dr. Church was well known here. The host took him to a private table in the back and took his hat and cane. A curly-haired girl arrived bearing a heavy tray. On it were roast squab, lamb chops, and a heap of plump sausages. Boiled potatoes, white beans, and cabbage were in separate bowls, and there were baked apples, too. A basket of johnnycake completed the menu.

Dr. Church ordered a bottle of claret. Oliver craved sausage, but his stomach rebelled. He ate lamb and potatoes, washed down with weak Bohea tea.

"What is the hardest part of your life, Carter?" asked the doctor once his wine had been poured.

Warmed by food and drink, Oliver spoke freely. "The hardest part for me is loneliness."

"Oh? What about little Hilde?"

Oliver studied his dinner. For almost two years he had been shunning friendships at every turn. He never knew who he could trust. If his part in the *Gaspee* affair became known, his life would not be worth a farthing.

Dr. Church tore a second squab apart with his fingers and repeated the question.

"Hilde is a fine girl."

"I knew you thought so. Have you kissed her yet?" Embarrassed, Oliver buried his face with his cup.

Dr. Church chuckled. "I see. Here I am trying to further your cause, and you're not doing your part!"

He had ordered Hilde to the dispensary for treatment, then arranged to be away while Oliver was there. He had set up other encounters, such as sending Hilde to nurse him during his illness.

"Is our Daphne still fleeing from young Apollo?" asked the doctor.

Oliver understood the analogy now. In some legends, Apollo was also the god of medicine.

"I thought gentlemen did not discuss such things."

"Of course, you are right." The subject of Hilde was exhausted when a woman approached the booth. She was very pretty, Oliver thought, with pale skin and vivid blue eyes set off by jet-black hair. Both of them stood to greet the lady.

"Benjamin," said the lady. "How good to see you."

"And you, madam."

She held out her hand, and the doctor kissed it. Oliver sensed this was not a chance meeting.

"It has been a long time," she chided.

Dr. Church spread his hands. "I labor like Hercules these days." He pointedly changed the subject. "Ah, forgive me! You two have not been introduced. Oliver Carter, this is Mrs. Lemon."

She held out her hand. Oliver merely grasped it and let go. She smiled warmly, and Oliver felt distinctly out of place. He remained standing when she sat down. He said good-night.

"How polite he is," Mrs. Lemon remarked. "Discrete too, I pray?"

"You may rely upon it," said the doctor. "Good-night, Carter."

Oliver walked slowly away from The Gambols, pondering what he had seen and heard. When he passed a nearby alley, someone shrank into the shadows, hoping to go unnoticed.

Oliver was sure he saw the skulker's face, streaked by a slim shaft of moonlight. It was Ezekiel Brown.

"Hello?" No one answered.

Brown was supposed to be in Raynham. Was he spying on the doctor? Who would want him to—Mrs. Church? He was Dr. Church's man, but outraged honor—and gold—could buy some men's allegiance.

It did not feel like a good idea to enter the alley. Better to mind his own business. Dr. Church's private life did not concern him.

Not two streets from The Gambols he was knocked down by a pack of boys running pell-mell down the lane. In a moment they were gone, racketing up the street and around the corner. Oliver was trying to get on his feet when the cause of their panic appeared: a party of redcoats!

"There's one!"

Although he had not done anything wrong, Oliver felt a stab of fear. Quickly ringed by soldiers, he was pinned to the wall by bayonets thrust against his chest.

"I've done nothing!" he protested.

"You're with those banditti—admit it!" shouted a soldier with corporal's stripes on his sleeve.

"I'm a respectable apothecary!"

The redcoats had been buying supplies outside the city, Oliver learned. On the way back to Castle William, their freight wagon had been set upon by youths. Two soldiers on the wagon had been battered unconscious by a barrage of stones. When soldiers of the escort turned to chase the attackers, the boys scattered.

With much cursing, Oliver was marched to the scene of the attack. There he saw a trampled soldier's hat and bloodstains on the street. Half a dozen redcoats stood around, leaning on their muskets. When Oliver's captors appeared a shout went up: "We got one! Here's one of them!"

Angry redcoats surrounded Oliver. They were soldiers of the 64th Regiment, just like the men Dr. Church treated for fighting at the Green Dragon Tavern. They shouted several accusations at Oliver: He had taunted the injured men and kicked the fallen soldiers when they were helpless.

Oliver denied everything. He repeated Dr. Church's name, hoping the doctor might have helped some of the soldiers. If anyone knew the doctor, maybe they would vouch for him.

A soldier hurled him to the ground. He tried to get up, but a musket butt drove him down again. It was only a glancing blow, but it was enough to send him sprawling. The ring of furious men closed in.

Oliver covered his head with his hands, expecting at any moment to be pounded to death by boots and muskets. Before any blows landed he heard a loud voice calling for order. He lifted his head enough to see a swarthy man on horseback parting the mob. His scarlet coat was faced with white. Gold epaulets perched on his shoulder.

"Make way, there, make way!" he cried. He drew his sword and swatted unruly soldiers. "Make way, I say!"

The soldiers drew back. Oliver staggered to his feet, grasping the bridle of the man's horse for support. It was a miracle—a redcoat officer happened on the scene at this time of night.

"I am Captain Cane," he said. "What is the meaning of this nonsense?"

The corporal who had seized Oliver tried to explain. Cane listened, growing more impatient with every word he heard.

"Dolt!" he said. "What proof do you have of his guilt?"

"We chased the rascals, sir," said the corporal. "When we caught up with them, this one was lagging behind."

Oliver explained who he was and why he was in the street when the soldiers found him.

"You're Dr. Benjamin Church's chemist?" asked Cane. Oliver swore he was. "Let me see your hands."

Oliver showed them both, front and back. Cane swore at the soldiers.

"Idiots! A man who has been in a fight doesn't have unmarked hands! Look!"

The redcoats were silent. Men at the edge of the crowd began to slip away.

Cane held out his hand to Oliver. "Come on, lad. I'll settle this for once and all."

Gratefully Oliver swung onto the officer's horse behind him. "Your colonel will be informed of this disorder," the captain said severely. "Recover your supplies and return to the fort at once!"

Cane spurred his horse and it trotted away. In short order, they were on Hanover Street, in front of the still, dark Church house.

"Rouse the doctor," Cane told Oliver. "If he vouches for you, that will be the end of it."

Oliver went, secretly afraid the doctor might be lingering at The Gambols. He knocked loudly many times before Dr. Church opened the door. He was wearing a long white nightshirt and carrying a half-lit candelabra.

"Carter? What the devil—?" Dr. Church saw the British officer in the street. "Good God, man, what have you done?"

Oliver hastily explained. Dr. Church frowned deeply.

"Wait here. Do not leave the doorstep for any reason."

Clad in his nightshirt, the doctor strode to the waiting captain. They had a short, animated conversation Oliver could not overhear. Dr. Church pointed at him and waved his free hand. Captain Cane nodded a few times, then rode away.

Dr. Church stalked back to his house. In passing, he snapped, "Go home, Carter!"

"Yes, sir. Thank you, sir."

"And, Carter!" Dr. Church paused in the doorway. "Say nothing of this incident to anyone, understand? Not anyone!"

Oliver was so relieved to get out of this predicament with his skin intact that he happily agreed. Dr. Church slammed the door shut.

chapter six

Threepence Per Pound

August 1773

Like leaves in an autumn wind, scraps of paper blew down Middle Street, catching at curbs or in doorways. Oliver clasped his coat close to his neck and bent into the wind, holding his hat on with his other hand. As he fought to reach Cross Street, he realized without irony that an even greater storm was brewing for the colonies.

Word of a new crisis had been building with every sail entering Boston harbor. Post riders from New York, Providence, and Philadelphia arrived with news of the latest outrage from Britain. As the leaflets blowing past Oliver's feet proclaimed, a new Tea Act had been passed by Parliament in May. The East India Company, which had a monopoly on the import and sale of tea in the British Empire, was in dire financial straits due to a glut of tea from India. Its warehouses bulged with unsold leaves. Many Americans refused to buy the East India Company's tea, which was unfairly taxed, preferring instead to buy smuggled Dutch tea—or drink no tea at all.

The East India Company's friends in Parliament cooked up a plan to save their business. They removed the regular tax on tea sold in the colonies. All that remained was the import duty of threepence per pound paid by colonial purchasers. How could the colonists object to that? After all, fine English Bohea tea was now cheaper than smuggled Dutch tea. Americans would save money buying British tea, and the great East India Company would be saved.

They could not have been more wrong. Everywhere there was great excitement about this new attempt to fill Britain's coffers with American money. In Boston, the Sons of Liberty met almost daily. Speakers reminded everyone how they had defeated the Stamp Act and the Townshend Acts. *No taxation without representation!* The slogan echoed in every street and tavern. Boston seethed with barely contained anger.

Oliver reached Cross Street. Wind swirled through alleys and over rooftops, plastering a blizzard of leaflets to his legs. He stamped his feet until the leaflets fell off.

Though it was only mid-afternoon, the lowering sky made the day as dim as sunset. Oliver opened the dispensary door. The wind caught it, hurling it against the wall. It snuffed out Dr. Church's candle and scattered his medical notes across the floor.

"Careful, Carter!" he said. Oliver quickly shut the door. While Dr. Church restored the candle, Oliver recovered the doctor's notes. He took a small packet out from inside his jacket. It was wrapped tightly with blue oilcloth and tied with twine. This he laid atop Dr. Church's notes.

"Here it is, sir."

Dr. Church took the packet. He slit the cord and unfolded the layers of cloth. Inside was a block of ivory-colored powder, pressed into a pillow-shaped cake. Dr. Church pinched off a tiny sample. He rubbed it between his fingers, then tasted it.

"Excellent quality opium," he said, smiling. "Bless the Dutchmen."

Oliver had been to Darby's Wharf to meet the barkentine *Jan Baltus*. He met the first mate, Ralf. The Dutchman had opium brought all the way from the Dutch East Indies. Oliver paid him with Dr. Church's gold and returned to the dispensary with the precious medicine.

As Dr. Warren had feared, the summer flux had turned deadly. Bostonians were dying daily. Mama Oleander, the old woman who ran Oliver's favorite tavern, the Saracen's Beard, succumbed in late July. So had Mr. Buckthorn, whose servant Mary Anne had been Oliver's first prescription in Boston. To halt the rampage, Dr. Church, Dr. Warren, and the rest of Boston's medical men needed strong medicine.

On Oliver's worktable Dr. Church cut the block of opium in half. He told Oliver to prepare laudanum tincture, one dram of opium per vial. Oliver carried the precious packet to his workbench and began weighing out the doses on his scale.

"I shall distribute the remainder among my colleagues," Dr. Church said. "Keep the door bolted until you have the doses mixed. It wouldn't be good to have you arrested for smuggling."

Thunder bellowed. The impact made Oliver's delicate scale tremble.

Dr. Church glanced skyward. "Jove signals his displeasure," he said, as if he could see the storm clouds through the wall. "I'd best wrap up."

He draped a long cloak around his shoulders. Oliver followed him to the door. Just as the doctor opened it, rain lashed Cross Street. Dr. Church grimaced. He put on his hat and reminded Oliver to bar the door.

Dr. Church dashed away, bowed against the downpour. Oliver slid the iron bolt shut. Wind rattled the door against it.

Glancing out the window, Oliver saw Dr. Church struggle up the street. The doctor hadn't gone twenty yards when another figure, wrapped in a dark coat, emerged from a doorway and fell in behind him. Rain on the diamond-shaped panes made it impossible to recognize the second man, but Oliver was sure from the size, shape, and posture it was Ezekiel Brown. For weeks he had caught glimpses of the family coachman lurking in alleys and doorways, watching Dr. Church. He had said nothing about it to the doctor. Oliver first assumed Brown was spying on the doctor for Mrs. Church. The doctor was well known for his love of wine, women, and song.

As the weeks went by, it seemed less and less likely that Mrs. Church would have had her husband shadowed so long. Brown could have summoned the missus back from Raynham weeks ago. She remained in Raynham, and Brown still shadowed the doctor.

Another possibility grew in Oliver's mind. Who else had a reason to keep track of the doctor's doings? The redcoats? The colonial authorities—or the Sons of Liberty?

Seized with curiosity, Oliver flung on his own foul-weather gear, a secondhand brown redingote with a patched hole in the shoulder. He blew out the candle and slipped out into the billowing storm.

Dr. Church had gone south on Middle Street. Blinking the rain from his eyes, Oliver peered around the corner. He saw the doctor hugging the east side of the street. His shadow was on the opposite side of the street about ten yards behind. Like his employer, Oliver hugged the leeward side. A time or two Brown glanced back. Each time Oliver turned away, as if walking in the opposite direction, or ducked into a doorway.

Not much happened until they reached the north end of Towne House square. Brown halted, stepping back into a convenient alley. Oliver chanced being seen to cross the street behind his quarry. From there he saw Dr. Church had halted on the corner of Queen Street.

It was clear why he stopped: Four mounted redcoats were crossing the square, riding alongside a supply wagon. Since the stoning of their men a few weeks ago, the army had begun escorting every wagon that passed through the city with dragoons. The soldiers had carbines propped against their thighs, imposing but useless in the rain.

Seeing the wagon, Dr. Church walked directly toward it. Oliver admired his nerve, passing a redcoat patrol with dangerous contraband in his pocket. He strolled by the mounted men, spoke to them briefly, then disappeared behind the Towne House.

Brown left his hiding place. Having lost the doctor, he didn't creep, but sprinted after his quarry. Oliver was obliged to jog after him.

The square was lashed by wind-driven torrents. Brown stopped in the middle of the street, turning this way and that. He was terribly conspicuous, but so far the dragoons ignored him. The coachman circled the Towne House until he spied Dr. Church proceeding down King Street. Before he could follow, two soldiers on horseback challenged Brown. He hesitated a moment, then fled up Cornhill Street, his ungainly feet kicking up great splashes as he ran. The redcoats laughed and did not pursue.

Oliver had no desire to be questioned by the redcoats again, so he returned to the dispensary and resumed weighing out the opium. Dividing out one dram doses took a long time. Night fell. He was still at his work when someone rattled the front door.

He covered his worktable with a cloth and went to the door with a candle. He saw a round face at the window, blurred by darkness and rain. It was his employer.

Oliver unbolted the door. Dr. Church burst in, stamping his sodden shoes. With a flourish, he flung off his soaked cloak.

"Good God, Carter, you're still here?" he exclaimed. The turned-up brim of his tricorn hat dribbled water when he removed it. "I thought you'd be at supper by now."

"I've not finished dividing the medicine."

"No?" Dr. Church went to the door and looked through at Oliver's table.

"I'll be finished soon, sir."

Dr. Church was about to leave when he saw Oliver's coat, hanging on a peg in the corner. It dripped on the plank floor.

He turned to Oliver. "You've been out."

"Yes, sir."

Dr. Church asked where he had been. Oliver had been weighing his answer ever since the doctor had returned.

"Sir, I followed you after you left this afternoon."

Dr. Church frowned. "Is that so? Why?"

"Because I saw a man at your heels, sir. I followed him."

The doctor's ire turned to surprise. "Someone was after me? Who?"

Oliver ran a hand through his damp red hair. "I know the man, sir. So do you. I've seen him several times this summer watching you from afar." Dr. Church demanded to know the spy's name.

"Ezekiel Brown. He dogged you as far as the Towne House, where some redcoats scared him away. That's when I came back, too."

The doctor did not scowl or laugh or utter any oaths. He looked as blank as a marble statue.

"You're certain, Carter? Brown is supposed to be in Raynham, carting my wife and daughters around the countryside."

Oliver catalogued the times and places he'd observed Brown trailing Dr. Church. The doctor listened, then went to his consulting table and sat down. He rubbed a finger absently across his lips.

"Sir?" Oliver said. Dr. Church answered with a grunt. "Why would your own coachman be following you around Boston?"

The doctor stared at him. "Carter, have you mentioned this to anyone else?" Oliver swore he had not. "Good. Don't breathe a word of this to a soul."

Dr. Church stood. "It's about time you understood something. Dr. Warren is more than a medical colleague. He and I are members of a special committee whose purpose is to guarantee the liberty of these American colonies—beginning with Massachusetts Bay, of course."

Oliver knew this, and said so. Dr. Church's presence on the committee was common knowledge.

"Because I count many Tories and government officials among my patients—and officers of the king's army—people speculate a great deal about my politics," Dr. Church went on. "My role in the Sons of Liberty is not widely known."

Dr. Church took out a small brass key. He unlocked the drawer of his consulting table and slid it open. From under a sheaf of medical papers he brought out a handful of printed pamphlets.

"These I wrote for the cause."

Oliver glanced over the booklets. One that caught his eye was titled *To Commemorate the Bloody Tragedy of the Fifth of March 1770.* It was an oration on the Boston Massacre, delivered on the anniversary of the killings.

There were other pamphlets, too. Some were lampoons on Tory politicians like Lord North and Lord Germain, and attacks on Governor Hutchinson of Massachusetts. This last was written in rhyme and read in part:

> The GOVERNOR at home did sip his Tyrant's tea,
> And dine on Beef and Fish,
> While PATRIOTS spoke a heartfelt Plea,
> For Liberty was their wish.

And so on, for many pages. Dr. Church's name did not appear anywhere on the poem ridiculing the governor. Oliver returned the papers to Dr. Church.

"Do you see?" he said. "My devotion to liberty has caused the government to set Brown to spy on me."

It made sense. Dr. Church was well connected to both sides. What he knew, and what he did, was bound to be of interest to the king's men.

"What will you do about Brown, sir?" Oliver asked.

"Do? Why, nothing." Seeing the young man's puzzlement, Dr. Church smiled slyly. "As long as I know Brown is a spy, I will be careful not to do anything compromising with him watching. I'll be more safe when I know he is not about."

This sounded dangerous to Oliver. When he expressed concern for the doctor's safety, Dr. Church replied, "Fear not, Carter. If the time comes I cannot operate safely under Brown's scrutiny, a word to the right people and he will cease to be a problem."

Oliver knew what he meant. One night the coachman would disappear. It had happened before in Boston.

chapter seven

A Good Round Hand

September and October 1773

As the summer faded, so did the deadly flux. The final toll was light, thanks to the efforts of the city's doctors. Governor Hutchinson sent personal congratulations to Dr. Church, Dr. Warren, and the rest of Boston's medical men for their work.

With the easing of the medical crisis, Oliver gained new duties as Dr. Church's secretary. He expressed his sympathy for the cause of liberty to the doctor, who offered to find Oliver a place with the Sons of Liberty. Oliver debated with himself for some time. Did he dare take up the cause again? As far as he knew, he was still wanted by the Crown for his part in the *Gaspee* affair. Dr. Church sensed his unease, though he did not know the truth about Oliver's past.

"Do as reason and your conscience command," he said. So Oliver did.

His handwriting had always been excellent. Oliver put his skill to work for the Sons of Liberty. He was called upon to

81

copy reports and transcribe letters for Dr. Church and other members of the committee.

He saw a great deal more of the men who led Boston's patriots. Mr. Revere remained generous and kind. Samuel Adams regarded Oliver with indifference, while Dr. Warren was polite but cool. He saw little of Mr. Otis, who was ill.

Oliver finally met John Hancock. He turned out to be a dapper man who couldn't seem to make up his mind if he was a radical, like William Molineux, or a philosopher of action, like Dr. Warren. Mr. Hancock took a liking to Oliver and paid him generously for delivering messages outside the city. Oliver protested he did not have to be paid to do his duty. Mr. Hancock brushed his objections aside.

"We give what we can to the cause, young man. You give your time and vigor. I have money, so that's what I give."

The cause was liberty for every American colonist. Liberty meant freedom—freedom from burdensome taxes, and freedom to speak and write as a person of conscience wished. The American colonies were ruled by ministers in London they did not choose, and they suffered under laws enacted by a parliament in which they had no elected representatives. As a result, rule from Britain was distant, arbitrary, and unfair.

Autumn brought another happy event. The Church family returned from Raynham, and Hilde with them. When Oliver first saw her, he was stunned by how much she had changed in one summer. Her apple-cheeks had slimmed to a gentle woman's face. Her hair had grown long. She wore it in a thick single braid, piled up in a bun at the back of her head. When Oliver saw her in the street in front of the Churches' house, he resolved there and then to marry her.

Dr. Church had sent Oliver to Hanover Street to help unload the family's possessions. He spent so much time chatting with Hilde that Lily said, "Why don't you two take your ease on the porch while I finish shifting these crates?"

Oliver apologized and went back to work in earnest. Embarrassed, Hilde set a wicker basket on her shoulder and hurried into the house.

Oliver noticed a stranger was unloading the Churches' carriage. Where was Ezekiel Brown?

"Run off," Lily replied. "Good riddance, I say. All summer the missus couldn't find him half the time. The day before we was to come home, he left, and we hasn't seen him since."

The man Oliver saw was only there to get the family home. He would be on his way back to Raynham by sundown.

Oliver carried a box of silver around to the scullery. Hilde was there, placing china cups in a cupboard.

"I'm glad you are back," he said, setting down the box.

"I am glad also."

"You'll be here from now on?"

"As long as the missus stays, so do I," she said, counting the teacups on her fingers.

She turned to the carton where the cups were nestled in a bed of straw. Her apron string caught one of the cups on the cupboard shelf. Before either of them could react, the delicate china smashed to bits on the brick floor.

Hilde and Oliver froze, staring at each other. Before Oliver could count to ten, Mrs. Church sailed into the room.

"What was that?"

Hilde went down on one knee and began picking up the shattered cup shards.

"An accident, Mrs. Church."

"You broke one of my French porcelain cups! Those were a wedding present! I ought to—"

Oliver blocked her path to the kneeling Hilde.

"I see," she said, eyes narrowing. "This is your doing. Distracting my maid, are you?"

"The doctor sent me to help unload the wagon," Oliver said. "And Hilde didn't break the cup. I did."

"Then you shall pay for it!"

He dug out what coins he had and slapped them on the table in front of her.

"If it is more than that, let me know," Oliver said coldly.

Faced with hard money, Mrs. Church didn't know what to say. Oliver took Hilde by the hand and urged her to rise. With grave dignity he said good day, and he left.

At the wagon, he told Lily what had happened. When she heard one of the missus's cups had been broken, she gasped.

"Did she beat poor Hilde?" asked Lily.

Oliver shook his head. "I said I broke it and paid her for it.

If anything happens to Hilde, I want you to tell me." Lily looked doubtful until Oliver slipped her a coin, his last.

"Please."

She rubbed the money between her thumb and forefinger, then gave it back to him. "Keep your money," she said. "Friends do things for friends."

"Thank you."

Hearing voices coming from the house, he hurried away. The Church daughters appeared at the front door, loudly demanding Lily bring their things into the house.

Oliver found a stranger waiting at the dispensary when he returned. It was Sunday, September 19, and Dr. Church did not have consulting hours that day. The stranger was not much older than Oliver, tall, rangy, with travel-stained clothes. Oliver headed him off by saying the doctor would not be in today to see anyone.

"I'm not here for medicine," said the fellow breathlessly. He thrust a rolled-up piece of paper into Oliver's hand.

"For the committee," he whispered. He walked away quickly, glancing back to see if he was being followed.

Oliver went inside. By the light of the front window he examined the paper. It was blank.

His first reaction was to throw it away, thinking the stranger was playing a prank. He was about to crumple it up when there was a knock on the back door of the dispensary. Hardly anyone used the back door. Curious, Oliver went through his workroom and put an ear to the panel.

"Who's there?" he said softly.

"Peter Hall."

Peter was the one-eyed fellow who worked at the Green Dragon. He'd been a sailor until he lost an eye to a tropical infection. Now he did odd jobs around the tavern, like washing dishes, sweeping, and tending the fires.

Oliver opened the door a crack. It was Peter. His eyepatch was in so deep it looked like it was embedded in his skull.

"The doctor wants you," he said.

He had wondered why Dr. Church was not at home supervising the return of his family. Oliver put on his jacket, and, as an afterthought, put the blank paper in his pocket.

The sky was washed clean of clouds, and a chill grew in the air. Oliver and Peter hurried through the empty streets to Green Dragon Lane. They entered the tavern, barely acknowledging the greetings of the regulars clustered around the fireplace. These were the same fellows who had once thought Oliver was a government spy.

Peter returned to the kitchen. Oliver ran upstairs to the room usually reserved for Masonic meetings. There he found Mr. Revere, Mr. Hancock, and Dr. Warren—but not Dr. Church. He misunderstood which doctor had summoned him.

"Ah, Carter, come in." Dr. Warren waved him forward. "A messenger is due anytime now with news from England. For reasons of secrecy he will not come here, but he may visit Revere's shop or Dr. Church's—"

"I saw him, sir!" Oliver blurted. "Not an hour ago! He left no message."

"What? Nothing at all?" asked Mr. Revere.

"He gave me a blank page as if it were an important letter."

Dr. Warren looked relieved. "Do you have the paper?"

He did, fortunately. Oliver handed it to the nearest man, Mr. Hancock.

"Blank all right," he said, studying both sides.

Dr. Warren held it up. The shutters were closed, darkening the room, but enough light came in through the window for the doctor to examine the paper minutely.

"There is sympathetic stain here."

Hancock said, "Invisible writing? How do we read it?"

Dr. Warren pulled over a thick candle on a stand. "The usual method is heat. Carter, fetch a brand from the fireplace."

Oliver went to the fire and used a fatwood splint to light the candle. Once lit, the doctor held the paper close to the flame, constantly moving it back and forth.

"Don't burn it," Mr. Revere warned.

Slowly at first, then with increasing speed, streaks of brown appeared on the paper. Oliver first thought the page had caught fire, then he saw the streaks formed writing.

Tea ships for America, it read. *To Boston, four:* Eleanor & Dartmouth *ships*, William & Beaver, *brigs. Consignees E & Hutchinson Jnr., Faneuil Jnr., J. Winslow, R. Clarke & Sons.*

"What does it mean?" Oliver asked.

"Shall I tell him?" said Dr. Warren. Hancock and Revere had no objections. "Parliament intends to tax all imported tea threepence a pound." This Oliver already knew. The news had been flying around Boston for weeks. "The East India Company has named those merchants to whom they will consign tea."

Dr. Warren pointed to the paper, now covered with blotchy brown letters. "'E & Hutchinson Jnr.' means Elisha and Thomas Hutchinson, Jr., are two of the merchants who will receive tea. They are the sons of the royal governor of Massachusetts, Thomas Hutchinson, Sr."

"'Faneuil Jnr.' is Benjamin Faneuil, Jr.," Hancock explained. "'J. Winslow' I assume is Mr. Joshua Winslow, and 'R. Clarke & Sons' is Mr. Richard Clarke's company." Mr. Revere and Dr. Warren agreed.

They gave Oliver the once-invisible message. He sniffed the scorched document.

"What did they use for the ink?"

"A solution of blue vitriol," said Dr. Warren offhandedly, noticing Oliver's professional curiosity. "Dr. Franklin is an expert on things besides lightning."

Oliver was holding a secret message sent by the great Benjamin Franklin. Franklin was the most famous American in the world—philosopher, author, publisher, printer, inventor, and diplomat. Even now he was in England pleading the colonies' cause in Parliament.

"The committee must be told," said Mr. Revere. "And the Loyal Nine." This was a name Oliver had not heard before.

"Send word around for a meeting tonight," Dr. Warren said. "Inform Mr. Adams first."

Oliver offered to inform Dr. Church about the meeting.

"Do that, Carter. We will meet here at eight o' clock," said Mr. Revere.

"You come, too," Dr. Warren said. "There may be correspondence to copy."

Oliver swallowed hard. The government would surely be on guard with a valuable cargo of tea coming. What would the Sons of Liberty do?

Oliver ran back to the dispensary. Dr. Church's carriage waited out front. A new coachman stood by the front wheel. He was a tubby, smiling little man in high boots. Seeing Oliver he tipped his hat.

"You'd be Carter, I daresay? My name is Beebe, Horatio Beebe. I am the new coachman."

Out of breath, Oliver tried to exchange polite greetings. Finally he gasped, "Is the doctor in?"

"I wouldn't be here otherwise, now would I?" said Beebe.

Inside, Oliver saw a light in his workroom and heard a commotion. From the workroom door he saw Dr. Church on his knees, rifling through papers scattered on the floor. They were prescriptions Oliver had filled, notes on how to make unfamiliar compounds, and so on. Dr. Church scanned the pages hastily, muttering under his breath.

"Sir?"

He looked up, face pale and wig askew. "Carter! Where the devil have you been?"

"I was summoned to the Green Dragon, sir."

"What for, pray?"

"A secret message has come from—" Oliver almost said "Dr. Franklin," but he checked himself and finished, "From England, sir."

Dr. Church stood up. "The messenger jumped ship before it docked, rowing ashore in a small boat. The harbor patrol spotted him, and taking him for a common smuggler, gave chase—"

"He was here," Oliver said, almost whispering.

Dr. Church seized Oliver by the lapel. "Did he give you anything?" Oliver nodded, but he didn't speak until the doctor released him.

"My apologies, Carter. The strain is very great . . . we're skulking under the gallows, you know."

He withdrew to the table, smoothing his waistcoat and powdered wig.

"What did he give you, Carter?"

Oliver told him how the man pressed a blank square of paper on him, and how Dr. Warren had deduced it contained a message penned in "sympathetic" or invisible ink.

"They read it in your presence? What did it say?"

"It names the ships bringing tea for Boston, and the men who will receive consignments of East India leaves."

"They'll be here in a month," Dr. Church said. "November, December at the latest. Then things will happen."

"What things, sir?"

Dr. Church looked away. "Dire things," he said quietly.

Oliver told him there was a meeting at eight at the Green Dragon. Carefully he asked if the doctor had ever heard of the Loyal Nine.

"Who mentioned them?" Dr. Church asked sharply. Oliver admitted it was Mr. Revere. "Keep clear of them, Carter, if you value your skin!"

"Who are they, sir?"

"Ruffians. Window smashers and tar boilers. When Samuel Adams has an enemy he wants to intimidate, he summons the Loyal Nine."

Oliver didn't dispute the doctor, but he found it hard to believe Dr. Warren or Mr. Revere would associate with common ruffians. On the other hand, the Sons of Liberty were known to have roughed up tax collectors before.

Dr. Church went out, not even apologizing for the mess he'd made.

Oliver picked up the disordered records of the last four and a half months of his life. He had intended to ask the doctor for permission to marry Hilde, but all thoughts of happiness had vanished when the mysterious stranger placed the folded paper in his hand.

chapter eight

The Loyal Nine

October 1773

Dr. Church had been in a foul mood all week, barking orders and keeping Oliver at work past sunset. In turns, Oliver was worried, then resentful, and finally understanding. The doctor was under great pressure. There were frequent meetings of the committee, many letters to compose and circulate, and unrest in the streets grew daily. Oliver went about his business constantly accosted by liberty men and loyalists alike, all demanding proof he supported their faction. He was able to talk his way past the Sons of Liberty by invoking his mentors. Paul Revere's name carried weight with the artisans, mechanics, and laborers of Boston.

Another worry for Dr. Church was the disappearance of Ezekiel Brown, though it seemed to bother Oliver more than it did the doctor.

"He's cowering in the castle, no doubt," the doctor said airily. He meant Castle William, the fort in Boston Harbor.

Many government officials, fearful of liberty mobs, had taken refuge at the fort.

On October 18 the *Boston Gazette and Country Journal*, the weekly newspaper that was the printed voice of the Sons of Liberty, broke the news about the tea shipments and the men who were supposed to receive it. Oliver read with more understanding than most Bostonians, but no less excitement:

> *It is the current Talk of the Town that Richard Clarke, Benjamin Faneuil, and the two young Messrs Hutchinson are appointed to receive the Tea allowed to be exported for this place. This new Scheme of Administration, lately said to be so friendly to the Colonies, is at once so threatening to the trade, and so well calculated to establish and increase the detested TRIBUTE, than an attempt to meddle with this pernicious Drug would render men much more respected than they are as obnoxious as were the Commissioners of stamped paper in 1765.*

The writer went on to say that the people of Boston, New York, and Philadelphia would destroy the tea rather than boycott it or force its return to England. He concluded with the veiled threat:

> *A correspondent has hinted that it would be highly improper to return those great Cargoes of Tea that are expected without sending the important Gentlemen whose existence depends on it along with it, to give the Premier the reasons for such conduct.*

Someone in the crowd reading this paper tacked to a post asked who "the Premier" was. A man wearing spectacles and a flat schoolmaster's hat explained the writer meant the prime minister of Great Britain, Lord North.

The topic of the tea coming to Boston was on everyone's mind. Not a day passed without a meeting, a handbill, or a demonstration about it somewhere in the city. Even Hanover Street was littered with leaflets when Oliver went to Dr. Church's house that evening. The bills reprinted the same blast he had seen in the *Gazette* earlier.

Oliver had spent several tedious hours gilding pills for one of the doctor's wealthy patients. Each tablet was covered with a whisper-thin sheet of gold leaf and nestled in a tiny rosewood box. Oliver had orders to deliver the finished pills no matter what the hour.

Feeling bold, Oliver went to the front door and banged the knocker. Lily answered his knock.

"My, aren't we taking on airs?" she said, seeing Oliver standing there, hat in hand. "Who may I say is calling?"

"Oh, let me in, Lily. I have some special pills the doctor asked me to make."

She held the door wide and curtsied when he entered.

"Stop it," he said. The house was quiet and the front rooms dark. "Is the family out?"

"Out and gone. That's why you got in the front door."

Oliver put the polished wooden box on a side table and made Lily promise to point it out to the doctor when he returned.

"Is—?"

"She's in the cookhouse," Lily said with a smirk. "Help yourself."

His short walk from the back door to the cookhouse was under a canopy of stars. Oliver's breath plumed from his lips. He entered the warm kitchen. Hilde looked up from her supper.

"Oliver!" she said, smiling.

He slipped onto the bench on the long side of the table. "How are you?"

"All is good." Hilde shifted a heavy cast iron pot toward him. He filled a wooden bowl with stew and tore some bread from the loaf cooling on the table.

She asked about his day. Oliver described rolling the gold pills. He ran them through the mill three times, then laid the white tablets on tiny squares of pure gold, hammered and rolled thin as a whisker. He had to tediously fold the gossamer sheets around each pill with a sable hairbrush. It was eye-popping work.

"Why wrap medicine in gold?" Hilde asked.

"Gold foil slows the release of the medicine in the pills over many hours."

"The only gold I ever see is when I polish the doctor's watch," Hilde said. "Three weeks it has been since money I have earned." Mrs. Church was still fining her for every mistake, large or small.

"A penny for scratching a silver bowl. Threepence for not

pressing gowns crisply enough. Twopence deducted for leaving streaks on a mirror. And so it goes."

Oliver slammed down his wooden spoon.

"This petty tyranny cannot go on!" What good did it do to fight the tyranny of Parliament and the colonial government when rules so unfair and arbitrary went unchallenged right where he lived?

"I will speak to Dr. Church about it."

"You must not! He will not always choose your part over the missus!"

"I'll take that chance. I've been meaning to speak to him anyway." Oliver took a deep breath. "I want to buy your freedom, Hilde."

She stared. "Why would you do that?"

"Because indentured servants cannot marry."

When he finally said it, Oliver felt as though a great length of chain had fallen from his shoulders.

All the color drained from Hilde's face. For a moment he thought she might faint. Oliver took hold of her hand.

"Do not jest with me," she stammered.

He held her cold fingers closely. "I am in earnest. Will you marry me, Hilde?"

Her mouth opened and closed a few times. Finally she managed to say, "No, Oliver."

Now it was his turn to gape. "But why?"

"I hardly know you." Hilde freed her hand. "And I could not marry a man who bought me like a horse at market."

He knew he had gone too far, too fast. Oliver tried to apologize.

"But," she said, "if I know you longer and come to love you, that is a different matter."

He would have agreed to almost any condition. When she smiled again, he asked her a very important question.

"What is your whole name? I don't know your family name at all."

"No one has asked me that in years," she said with pride. "I am Anna-Maria Gunhilde Meers. To all I am 'Hilde,' for only my father and mother called me Anna-Maria."

"I'm glad to meet you, Miss Meers."

When Lily entered a short time later, Hilde and Oliver were laughing.

"Glad to hear some happiness 'round here," she said, heaping soiled linen on the floor in preparation for washing it. "The master and the missus haven't been too friendly of late." Hilde rolled her eyes emphatically. Oliver asked about all of the trouble.

Mrs. Church wanted to entertain more in Boston, but Dr. Church had forbidden it. He was identified with the cause of liberty, and he didn't dare play host to the redcoat officers and royal officials Mrs. Church counted as her friends. That did not sit well with Hannah Church. She berated her husband and his politics. She demanded he leave "those radical ruffians," as she called them, and return to the society of loyal subjects of the king.

"The doctor wouldn't hear of it," Lily declared.

Hilde said, "He said his fortune lay with the Whigs, even if it did not come from them."

Oliver stopped eating. He asked Hilde to repeat what she said. She did, apologizing for her poor English.

"Your English is fine," he assured her. What did Dr. Church mean?

At that moment, a runner arrived from Dr. Williamson's, where the Churches had gone to a dinner party. The Churches would be back within the hour. They wanted the beds turned down and fires lit in their bedrooms.

Lily and Hilde went back to the house. Oliver had to clear out. He lingered at the cookhouse door, yearning for some sign from Hilde. It was too much to expect a kiss, but a smile could satisfy him for days. In a hurry, Hilde brushed by without a second glance. Oliver was stricken. Lily patted his cheek as she passed.

"Don't give up," she said. "You'll hook that fish yet."

It was a cold walk home. He had not lost all hope, but Oliver feared Hilde would not be able to free herself from the spiteful Mrs. Church. What could he do? While wrestling with the problem in his head, two men appeared out of the dark. They fell in step on either side of him.

"Are you Carter the apothecary?"

Warily, he admitted he was. "What do you want with me?"

"The nine want you."

Oliver halted. "What 'nine' do you mean?"

"The loyal ones," said the other man. He gestured politely for Oliver to follow him. Oliver knew it was not a request but a command. Wary but excited, he went with the men.

They went straight to Hanover Square, near the Liberty Tree. At this hour, the streets were vacant, and the men took him to Chase & Speakman's distillery on the other side of the square. Chase & Speakman made rum.

Inside, the air was hot and strong with the smell of alcohol. Two African men tended a large copper boiler, while a stillmaster in his shirtsleeves shook a few drops of rum in a clear bottle to see how it beaded on the glass. Oliver knew that was a test of alcohol strength. His guides prodded him to a back staircase. Up he went until he found a bolted door. One man rapped a special pattern of knocks on the door. A wicket opened. Seeing who was there, the porthole was closed and the bolt drawn back.

Beyond was a good-sized room, lined on three sides with rum barrels. A plank table filled the rest of the room. Around this were seated several men. Oliver only recognized the face of Samuel Adams.

"Is this the lad?" said the man at Mr. Adams's right hand.

"That's him, the apothecary. He's all yours."

Adams stood up, shook hands with the others, and went out, passing Oliver without a word.

"My name's Avery," said the man who had spoke with Adams. "I'm told you have a fine, round hand, and you're a good liberty man."

"I am," Oliver replied, relieved.

"We have some letters we need copied." The original text of one was written by Samuel Adams, and the other was by Mr. Avery. To prevent the government and redcoats from recognizing their authorship, they needed someone to transcribe the letters. The copy could then be sent to a printer to be made into a leaflet or to a newspaper like the *Boston Gazette*.

Oliver removed his jacket and sat down at the table. Ink and a sharp quill were laid out for him. He picked up a long sheet of paper on which was scrawled a lengthy address, with many corrections, words crossed out, and others added in.

"Go on," said Avery. "Get to it."

Oliver dipped his pen and started to write. Phrases leaped off the page as he read ahead of what he was writing. The letter was apparently directed at the merchants who had agreed to sell the East India Company's tea in Massachusetts:

> . . . *you need not be surprised to find the eyes of ALL now fixed on you, as on men who have it in their power to ward off the most dangerous stroke that has been meditated against the liberties of America. . . . The Stamp and Tea Laws were both designed to raise a revenue and to establish* parliamentary despotism *in America. . . .*
>
> *You cannot believe that the Tea Act, with respect to its design and tendency, differs in one single point from the Stamp Act. If there be any difference, the* Tea Act *is the more dangerous . . . the duty, being paid on importation, is afterwards laid on the article, and becomes so blended with the price of it that, although every man who*

*purchases tea imported from Britain must of course pay
the duty, yet every man does not know it, and may,
therefore, not object to it. . . .*

*If Parliament can of right tax us 10 pounds for any
purpose, they may of right tax us 10,000, and so on,
without end. And if we allow them a fair opportunity of
pleading precedent by a successful execution of the Tea
Act, under your auspices, we may bid adieu to all that is
dear and valuable amongst men.*

Feeling the strength of the words, Oliver wrote faster and
faster, until his quill was flying over the page. When he
finished, he breathed hard and his face was flushed.

"This will give the Tories something to think about! How
shall it be signed?"

Avery shrugged. The other members of the Loyal Nine
consulted with one another. By listening, Oliver quickly noted
their names: Mr. Welles, Mr. Bass, Mr. Chase (owner of the
distillery, and their host), Mr. Edes, Mr. Trott, Mr. Smith, Mr.
Cleverly, and Mr. Crafts. Mr. Welles, a portly man with a ruby
nose, supplied the signature. He took the pen from Oliver and
wrote with a flourish at the bottom SCAEVOLA.

"That should tweak our erudite governor and his friends!"
he said.

"Who is Scaevola?" asked Oliver.

"A hero of the Roman Republic who faced down the threat
of tyranny to his country," said Mr. Welles.

Mr. Edes took the paper. As publisher of the *Gazette*, he
promised to run the letter in the next edition. Oliver was

puzzled. If Edes was a member of the Loyal Nine, why go to all the trouble of recopying the letter? He could simply burn the original once it had been printed, and deny the authorities any access.

"At a trial, lack of evidence is sometimes more damning than one hundred confessions," Mr. Welles said sagely. "It implies an incriminating fact has been deliberately suppressed." Although no one said so, from that moment, Oliver decided Mr. Welles must be a lawyer.

The letters done, the solemn members of the Loyal Nine relaxed and became quite friendly. A rum keg was tapped. Oliver politely refused a dram of spirits.

"Would you prefer tea?" asked Mr. Avery, with mock severity.

"I like tea." The friendly mood froze until Oliver added, "But I prefer cider."

chapter nine

"O.C., Secretary"

O ctober passed in a blur. By day Oliver mixed elixirs and rolled pills for Dr. Church. In the evening, he was at the Green Dragon or at Chase & Speakman's, transcribing broadsheets or copying letters. He copied reports, which were sent by rider to towns in Massachusetts and to points beyond like Providence, New York, and Philadelphia.

One night at the end of October, Oliver was at the Green Dragon as usual. A sheaf of papers came in from the Loyal Nine. They were short notes, only a few dozen lines. Dr. Warren and Dr. Church looked them over before passing them to Oliver to copy.

"Use your best hand, lad," Dr. Church said. The note was a summons written by Mr. Avery to the tea merchants expecting shipments from England. Oliver would long remember the words:

> *The Freemen of this Province understand, from good authority, that there is a quantity of tea consigned to your*

house by the East India Company, which is destructive to the happiness of every well-wisher to his country. It is therefore expected that you personally appear at the Liberty Tree on Wednesday next, at twelve o' clock at noon day, to make a public resignation of your commission, agreeable to a notification of this day for that purpose. Fail not, upon your peril.

"This is final," he said, startled by the harsh tone.

Dr. Warren agreed. "It is for the consignees to decide whether they are slaves or free men."

Oliver took a deep breath and began the first of seven copies. As he finished each one, one of the doctors would whisk it away. When he completed the last one, Oliver put down his pen and flexed his cramped fingers.

Dr. Church noticed the letters were unsigned.

"What are those initials Avery uses?" Dr. Warren said, furrowing his brow. In the firelit room his blond hair and white waistcoat seemed to glow with a light of their own.

"'M.Y.,'" Dr. Church said idly. A faint smile crossed his lips. He bent over the table, took the first copy of the letter to the tea merchants and signed it "O.C., Sec'y."

"Sir!" Oliver protested.

Dr. Warren was not amused. "You should not use Carter's initials."

"Why not?" Dr. Church said. "It gives him a place in history."

"It may put his neck in a noose."

"Nonsense!" Dr. Church got a second note and signed it

like the first. "The handwriting of the signature is mine, not his. Besides, who would credit a young apothecary, not yet twenty, as the author of such seditious missives?"

Having signed them all, Dr. Church instructed his journeyman to fold and seal the letters.

"Sir, my initials—" Oliver was so astonished he could not continue his work.

"Fear not, lad. Sometimes the best disguise is to lie in plain sight."

"This is serious business, Benjamin," Dr. Warren said.

Smiling, Dr. Church replied, "So it is. If we undertake to defend our liberties with light hearts, how can we fail to face down our grim ministerial foes?"

Early on November 2, 1773, the letters with Oliver's initials were delivered to the tea importers. Richard Clarke sent his note to General Haldimand. His intelligence officer, Major Cane, set out to find out who wrote the O.C. letters. Every informer in Boston was alerted to be on the lookout for clues to the author of the threatening letters.

Oliver was at work the next morning when he heard church bells ringing. He went to the consulting room. Dr. Church was examining the mashed fingers of a dockyard carpenter.

"They're summoning everyone to the Liberty Tree," Dr. Church said, bandaging the workman's hand. Oliver looked at the wall. The shadow touched eleven. The meeting was called for noon.

"Are you going, sir?"

"No," said Dr. Church irritably. "Can't you see I have patients to treat?"

Five were waiting at the door. Nevertheless, Oliver chafed at remaining behind. He was anxious to see if any of the tea merchants would turn up at the Liberty Tree.

"Oh, go on," said the doctor in better humor. "I'll get no work out of you if you don't." Oliver was at the door in a flash. "Mind you, don't get your head broken! You have medicines to make this afternoon!"

Oliver promised to be careful. Then he was outside in the autumn sun, cramming his hat on his head. The nearer he got to the Liberty Tree, the thicker the streams of people became. When he reached the square, several hundred Bostonians were already there, with more arriving every minute. Oliver didn't know what the tea merchants looked like, but he assumed they were gentlemen of substance, and no one like that was present.

The crowd swelled to five hundred, all laborers, tradesmen, and idlers. To Oliver's surprise, no one from the committee appeared to address them. He could not imagine why Mr. Adams or Dr. Warren didn't exhort the expectant mob on the usual themes of liberty and justice. The noon hour came and went.

What's this humbug, people began to ask? Where are the tea merchants? Where are the Sons of Liberty?

Finally they came. Oliver saw Dr. Warren at the edge of the crowd, which parted respectfully for him. With him was

William Molineux, who had roused the crowd the first time Oliver visited the Liberty Tree. He was a loud, red-faced bully. He had once cornered Oliver in the Green Dragon and harangued him for half an hour about British injustices in Ireland. He assumed Oliver, being of Irish descent, was as outraged as he was. It took direct intervention by Mr. Revere to save Oliver from further ranting.

The crowd gave a cheer when Dr. Warren and the others joined them. No one cheered a moment later when a carriage entered the square. Thinking a tea merchant had come at last, the mob surrounded the coach, shouting "Liberty!" and "No taxation!" They were disappointed when Dr. Church emerged. Standing on the step, Dr. Church raised his hat to the crowd.

"Liberty!" he cried. He had an oddly amused look on his face. "Liberty for all!"

Now the mob milled about, eager for action.

Molineux bellowed, "Since the high and mighty tea merchants will not lower themselves to answer the summons of the people, the people should go to them and demand their submission to our will! They are all at Clarke's counting house!" he cried. "You know the place, at the bottom of King Street! Follow me, liberty men! Follow me for freedom!"

With a roar the crowd filled in behind Molineux, Dr. Warren, and Dr. Church. What an odd company they made. Two doctors, one brilliant, one worldly, and a blustering shopkeeper—a love of liberty made for strange fellowships.

At Richard Clarke's warehouse, the entrance was barred by Clarke's workmen. They blocked the doors, standing in the way with arms folded and faces grim. The mob flowed up to the walls of the warehouse and stopped. There was some discussion at the door, and a delegation of nine was admitted: Dr. Warren, Dr. Church, Molineux, and six others went inside. Oliver did not get in. He caught Dr. Church's eye as he passed into the wide warehouse doors, but the doctor passed on without a word or a wave.

Oliver later heard from Dr. Church what had happened. Inside they found Mr. Clarke and his fellow tea merchants, Thomas Hutchinson, Jr., one of the governor's sons, Joshua Winslow (a very ill man, the doctor said), Benjamin Faneuil, Jr., and Richard Clarke's son, Isaac. Also present was Judge Nathaniel Hatch. At once, Molineux began shouting, trying to bully the merchants into refusing their commission to import tea. Mr. Clarke, with the support of the others, rejected Molineux's demands without hesitation.

Molineux told them darkly, "Since you have refused our most reasonable demands, you must expect to feel the utmost weight of the people's resentment!"

The delegation left. When the crowd realized the merchants had refused to give up their tea, a cry went up, "Out with them! Out with them!"

They surged for the warehouse doors, still ajar. Clarke's men, joined by the elderly Judge Hatch, tried to shut them out. There was a struggle.

Judge Hatch shouted, "In His Majesty's name, I order you to desist and disperse!" The liberty men jeered and simply pushed harder.

Oliver did not join the first rush to the doors. His heart was with the cause of liberty, but he was wary of violence. Memories of the *Gaspee* were never far from his mind.

A new surge from behind him propelled him unwillingly into the fray.

"Take the doors off their hinges!" someone cried.

The mob drew back. Clarke's men heaved the doors closed. Liberty men drew mallets and spikes from their work aprons and easily knocked the doors' hinge pins out. The double doors fell to the ground with a crash. With a hurrah, the mob pushed into Clarke's warehouse. Judge Hatch and the tea merchants bolted themselves in an upstairs office. Two dozen of Clarke's sturdiest employees faced several hundred liberty men. Clarke's men were armed with table legs, walking sticks, and similar improvised weapons. As the mob stormed the steps, Clarke's men met them halfway down the stairs.

There was much shoving and shouting. Skulls and fingers were whacked. Oliver was three ranks back from the fighting. He could not advance or retreat. Unarmed, he could only join in the general heaving match. Clarke's men fought stubbornly. All the while the overloaded stairs creaked and groaned. Fearing the steps would collapse, the liberty men began melting away, starting with those farthest from the action. The pressure on Oliver's back eased, then he found himself without anyone behind him at all.

"Give way! Give way!" was the cry now. The liberty men backed down the stairs. Molineux was at the foot of the steps, trying to rally them, but there were too many bruised heads to inspire any heroism.

In the street, the protestors tried to besiege the warehouse, but their hearts were not in a drawn-out struggle. Time passed, and the crowd shrank to under one hundred. Richard Clarke and his colleagues decide to brave the reduced crowd and leave. Aside from much bluster, insults, and fist shaking, no one attacked them.

Oliver watched the stern-faced Clarke march up King Street with the others close behind him. Across the street, he spotted Dr. Church sitting in his carriage. The doctor nodded politely to the merchants and was coldly snubbed. Dr. Church thumped the roof with his cane, and his new coachman, Beebe, drove away without offering Oliver a ride.

Aside from some sore muscles and a bruise or two, Oliver wasn't hurt. Back at the dispensary, he rubbed arnica into his limbs to ease the pain. There was a short, urgent knock on the back door.

Peter Hall from the Green Dragon appeared. Had Oliver been home long? How had he returned from the Clarke warehouse? By what route? Annoyed by the questions, Oliver replied that he had flown home, like a pigeon.

"You may wish you had," said Peter. "A man was killed today behind Clarke's warehouse."

"Killed? Who?"

"A liberty man. Brown, his name was. 'Zekiel Brown."

Brown had been found in an alley on the harbor side of the warehouse, stabbed in the back. As Dr. Church often did postmortems for the city, he had been summoned to examine the man's body. He found that Brown had died in late afternoon, after the mob had dispersed.

"Do you think the tea merchants killed him?" asked Peter.

Oliver had no idea. He did not mention what he knew about Brown's spying on Dr. Church. Later, Oliver asked Dr. Church about having Brown "taken care of." Church looked at his apothecary with great surprise.

"Do you know the oath of Hippocrates, the sacred vows all doctors take? I have sworn to preserve life, not take it."

His righteous objection did not ring true. Oliver's suspicions worsened when he realized the Sons of Liberty chose not to exploit Brown's death. If Tories, or hired toughs in the pay of the tea merchants, had killed a liberty man, the Sons of Liberty would have raised a great uproar. They did not. More puzzling still, the government and the redcoats did nothing about it all. It was as if Ezekiel Brown mattered to no one.

chapter ten

Watchword: Vigilance

November 1773

Tears flowed the day the Church family left Boston. Carriage and wagon were drawn up in the street, and laborers shuttled in and out of the house, carrying bundles and boxes. Dr. Church's daughters wept loudly.

"We shall miss all the winter parties!" the younger girl wailed.

"No dances, no Christmas fetes, no feasts! The country is a cemetery this time of year! No one of quality will be there!" the older daughter cried.

Their lamentations were in vain. Mrs. Church oversaw the upheaval of her family with grim resolution. Because of all the demonstrations and riots, Boston was no place for decent, law-abiding subjects of His Majesty. They were off to Raynham, and that was that.

Once again, Dr. Church did not go with his family. Oliver found him in his front room, wrapped in a burgundy dressing gown, sipping mulled wine. The doctor was reading the latest issue of the *Gazette* while his wife shouted orders at the laborers, threatening dire punishment if they broke a single piece of her china.

"Sir, there are several patients waiting at the dispensary," Oliver said.

The doctor traded his wine cup for a slice of buttered toast. "How many?"

"Six when I left. They may have left by now."

"Then there's no need to hurry, is there?"

He rose, dropping the paper in his chair. "I shall return shortly." He strolled out, hands thrust in his pockets.

Oliver picked up the *Gazette*. On Friday, November 5—today—a meeting was called at Faneuil Hall at ten o'clock to discuss the tea crisis. Oliver glanced at Dr. Church's mantle clock. It was half past nine. He wondered if Dr. Church was dawdling at home so he could attend the assembly.

Hannah Church stormed into the room. "Benjamin!" she exclaimed, but saw only Oliver standing there. "Where is the doctor?" she asked coldly.

"Dressing, ma'am."

She stalked out. He heard her utter a few harsh words in the hall and knew Hilde must be there. Once Mrs. Church's footsteps thumped up the stairs, Oliver peeked into the hall. Hilde was loading pewter candlesticks into her apron.

"Hello, Hilde."

She gave him the merest glance. "Good morning." She struggled with the heavy sticks. Oliver rushed to her aid, catching one weighty holder before it hit the floor.

"*Himmel!*" she sighed. "The world has gone mad!"

She preceded him back to the scullery. There Lily stuffed items into crates lined with straw. Seeing Oliver she said, "Make yourself useful!"

A stack of plates sat on the counter. At Lily's direction, Oliver carried them to a box and set them gently inside.

"Are you off to Raynham?"

Lily nodded, counting silver. "A dull, drafty place to be in winter," she said. Oliver asked when they would be coming back to Boston.

"Who knows? When Boston isn't crazy anymore!"

Men came to remove the crate. Lily directed them to protect the walls from the hard corners of the box. On the way out, she caught Oliver's eye and winked.

He had a few minutes. To Hilde he said, "On Christmas, I will come to Raynham to see you."

She pushed stray strands of hair out of her face. "How can you? It is far."

"Not so far. What would you like for Christmas? What gift can I bring to you?"

Hilde half smiled. "Since we are dreaming, I would dearly love some gingerbread."

"I'll find some, if I have to send to Pennsylvania for it," Oliver vowed. Hilde didn't answer. Oliver circled around the crate she was filling and saw tears on her cheeks.

"I don't want to go!" she said with sudden fervor.

"It's only until this tea business is settled. Maybe you'll be back before Christmas."

He laid a hand lightly on her shoulder. To his surprise she clasped his hand warmly. Then Lily returned, and Hilde broke away quickly.

"The doctor is asking for you," Lily said.

Oliver gave the African woman a hug. "Keep your good eye on everything." Lily promised she would.

He wanted to give Hilde a similar farewell, but he didn't dare. All he could do was say, "Farewell. I'll remember the gingerbread."

Dr. Church, somber in black, waited at the front door. Mrs. Church was with him. As Oliver approached, the doctor leaned toward his wife and kissed her on the cheek. It was a strangely cool gesture. Oliver's moment with Hilde, a mere handclasp, seemed an epic of love compared to the Churches' parting.

"Come, Carter. Work awaits."

They went out together into the crisp November air. Dr. Church ordered Beebe to take them to Faneuil Hall.

"You're attending the assembly?" Oliver said, pleased.

"I am. The suffering masses of Boston can spare us a little while longer."

The crowd at the hall was easily a thousand people or more. The meeting was called to order by John Hancock, who had been chosen to moderate the assembly.

More than a month ago, a set of resolves had been drawn up in Philadelphia about the colonies' rights and their duty to resist Parliament's unjust taxes. The tax on tea was mentioned in no uncertain terms.

Mr. Hancock read the words to the crowd: "'That whoever shall, directly or indirectly, countenance this attempt, or in any wise aid or abet in unloading, receiving, or vending the tea sent or to be sent by the East India Company, while it remains subject to the payment of a duty here, is an enemy of America!'"

The assembly roared its approval. Hancock held up a hand to quiet the room.

"The last resolve is: 'Be it resolved, that a committee be immediately chosen to wait on those gentlemen who, it is reported, are appointed by the East India Company to receive and sell said tea, and request them, from a regard to their own characters, and the peace and good order of this Town and Province, immediately to resign their appointments.'"

The crowd voted by voice to accept the resolutions. That done, Dr. Church left for his dispensary. Where his mood earlier had been cool, even smug, he seemed quite thoughtful as they rolled through the streets.

"Will the tea merchants give in?" Oliver asked.

"Would you?" the doctor replied. "If every penny you owned and your reputation as a businessman were tied up in this trade, would you back down? It isn't just to the East India Company these men owe their steadfastness. It's to the Crown and Parliament, too."

Dr. Church was correct. The Clarke family, Faneuil, Jr., and Winslow rejected the Philadelphia resolves. To accept them, they replied by letter to the town meeting, would mean a great loss of money and an even greater loss of confidence from their trading partners.

Since the attempt to storm Richard Clarke's warehouse, the streets of Boston resounded with demonstrations. Governor Hutchinson tried to keep order, but his council calmly resisted his effort to stifle the anti-tea protests. Pressured by the royal governor to do something, the council voted to ask the attorney general of the colony to prosecute anyone connected to the riot at the Clarke warehouse. It was a deliberately empty gesture. No one would be prosecuted because no one involved in the riot would be identified. Patriots were silent on that score, and Tories were too intimidated to testify.

The council's vote was the last straw for weary Governor Hutchinson. He wrote to his superiors in London that he no longer had any power in Massachusetts. The colony was now in the hands of the people, led by Samuel Adams and the Sons of Liberty.

Fearing more violence, redcoats of the 64th Infantry Regiment, stationed at Castle William in Boston Harbor, were ordered to make frequent marches through the city to discourage any trouble. Admiral Montagu, commander of the Royal Navy in American waters, brought his flagship, the mighty sixty-four-gun *Captain*, to Castle William, too, along with two frigates. The warning to Boston was clear.

Despite the growing unrest, Dr. Church's dispensary remained calm. Oliver's apothecary work dwindled to merely keeping the doctor's medicine cabinet filled. Neither said much to the other.

At sundown a few days later, Dr. Church consulted his pocket watch.

"I am off to supper," he announced.

Beebe arrived with the carriage and took Dr. Church away. It was raw and cold when Oliver made his way to the Green Dragon a little later. A steaming mug of cider was put in his hand without his having to ask for it. Dr. Warren was not present, but Mr. Revere was, along with Mr. Avery of the Loyal Nine, and the blustering Mr. Molineux.

"The *Hayley* has passed the light," Mr. Revere said straight off.

Hayley, Oliver was told, was one of John Hancock's ships. On board was Jonathan Clarke, son of Richard Clarke and one of his father's partners in the shipping business.

"Young Clarke will have instructions from his masters in London," Mr. Revere went on. "He'll stiffen the old man's back against us."

"He needs to know where things stand in Boston," Avery said, rising from his seat.

Molineux laughed harshly. "Leave that to me. I can fill the streets with chickens on an hour's notice." "Chickens" were street brawlers who fought for the Sons of Liberty.

"Let's find out what Mr. Adams has to say about it first," Mr. Revere said. The fight at Clarke's warehouse had not gone well. Another failure and the merchants and their allies would bring the hated tea ashore when it came, threats or no threats.

A few nights later, the Chickens struck. Oliver was not there, but he heard about it. A band of liberty men armed with whistles and horns formed in front of Mr. Clarke's house on School Street. Blowing their instruments, they quickly gathered a noisy mob of supporters. One of Clarke's neighbors came outside to try to convince the crowd to leave. While he was speaking, a piece of firewood was thrown at the mob from the Clarke house. Angry, the crowd brushed aside the neighbor and beat on Clarke's front door.

The Clarke family was celebrating Jonathan's return from London. When the patriots began pounding on the door, the Clarke women fled upstairs for safety. With the women went Isaac Clarke, Richard Clarke's younger son.

Arming himself, he opened an upstairs window and shouted down to the mob, "You rascals! Begone, or I'll blow your brains out!"

To emphasize his threat, he fired a pistol into the air. The shot enraged the crowd. For two hours they hurled rocks at the Clarke house, tore off the shutters, and trampled the yard. After terrifying the Clarkes, the mob dispersed.

The Clarkes were unharmed, but after experiencing two riots on his property, the elder Clarke had seen enough. With the other tea merchants he sent a petition to Governor Hutchinson, asking him to take over responsibility for the tea shipments. The merchants rightly feared the Boston mob would wreck their homes and businesses if the tea landed.

The governor could do nothing. His council was divided among Tories and liberty men, so he had little authority left. In despair, Richard Clarke gave up. Like Dr. Church's family, he chose to leave Boston and retire to his country house.

November was fast fading. One night near the end of the month, Oliver heard unusual noises downstairs. He descended the steps, candle in hand, ready to defend the dispensary from thieves.

Instead of bandits, he found Dr. Church seated at his consulting table.

"Oh, Carter. I am sorry I disturbed you."

He looked very unhappy. There were stacks of gold coins on the table, a lot of them. Oliver had never seen so many sovereigns at one time.

"Sir, is there a problem?"

"No trouble, Carter. I have received several payments for my services."

The doctor didn't make that much gold in a year. While trying to make sense of what he was seeing, Oliver sensed a presence in the shadows by the front window. A woman lingered there, clad in a long, dark cloak. Her face caught the dim candlelight—Mrs. Lemon.

Dr. Church saw the recognition on Oliver's face. He gruffly ordered him back to bed.

"It's just business, Benjy," Mrs. Lemon said. "No need for shame."

"Shame is for small men," Dr. Church replied loftily. He raked the gold into a dark suede purse.

"Mrs. Lemon has been my patient for some time," he said. "I have carried her on account, and now she has paid in full."

"Mrs. Lemon is very generous."

"Go to bed, Carter," the doctor said crossly.

Oliver crept back to bed. He heard them talking awhile, but they were careful not to speak too loudly. Before long he heard the front door of the dispensary open and shut.

With great care he went downstairs again. The doctor and Mrs. Lemon were gone. Oliver tried the doctor's table drawer. It was locked. Frustrated, he gave the drawer pull a hard shake. Something fell, ringing loudly on the floor.

It was one of the gold coins Mrs. Lemon had given Dr. Church. By the light of his fluttering candle Oliver saw that it was brand new, minted this very year.

A cold sensation of dread flowed over him. He had been in Boston long enough to know no one paid their debts in brand-new sovereigns—no one but Governor Hutchinson perhaps, or General Haldimand, commander of His Majesty's forces in North America.

chapter eleven

The Wrong Host

On November 28, 1773, the upstairs room of the Green Dragon was packed. The merchant ship *Dartmouth* had arrived off Boston at ten o' clock the night before. Not until six the next morning—a Sunday—could *Dartmouth* follow the tide into Boston harbor. Her captain anchored *Dartmouth* by Castle William, behind Admiral Montagu's flagship, HMS *Captain*.

Word flashed ashore. The Sons of Liberty had eyes everywhere, and they knew about the tea ship from the moment a pilot was sent to her. Oliver heard the news shouted in the street when he emptied his chamber pot early Sunday morning. Word quickly reached Governor Hutchinson, too, and General Haldimand was informed.

At the tavern, everyone from the committee able to be there was there. So were the Loyal Nine. Oliver was jammed against the back wall along with other couriers and clerks.

"It's very clear what must be done," Samuel Adams said, quieting the room without raising his voice. "The tea cannot now be sent back to England unless the duty is paid." Men grumbled and cursed at the mention of the tax. "Nor can it be unloaded without paying the tax."

"Can Governor Hutchinson order the tea to another Massachusetts port?" asked Mr. Avery.

Adams shook his heavy head. "The Acts of Trade, which our governor took an oath to enforce, does not allow an anchored vessel to leave without a pass signed by the governor." He smiled darkly. "And he cannot issue a pass unless the duty is paid, or else he's no better than a smuggler."

"Here, here!" said Dr. Warren, raising his cup to Mr. Hancock. The wealthy merchant scowled, and a laugh circled the room.

"So the tea is trapped," Mr. Edes said.

"They have twenty days in which to pay the required tax," Mr. Adams went on. "Twenty days from last night is—"

"December seventeenth," Mr. Avery calculated quickly.

Everyone took turns speculating what the governor would do. Dr. Church cleared his throat.

"Is it true that Castle William is not considered to be Boston proper? For trade purposes, I mean?" he said.

That silenced the room.

"Do you mean, if the *Dartmouth* remains at the fort, it can legally return to England?" said Mr. Welles.

Startled, the lawyers present agreed. Castle William was His Majesty's property—not part of the city.

"We must get that ship to anchor at the Long Wharf!" Mr. Adams said.

Oliver was confused. The Sons of Liberty had long demanded the tea not be brought to America. Now their leaders were trying to keep it. Gathering his nerve, Oliver voiced his confusion to the committee.

Mr. Adams looked over the heads of the seated men at Oliver. "We mean to force the issue, young man. We've whipped the town into a fury over unjust taxes. If the tea goes back, the support of many good Bostonians will go with it." Mr. Adams wanted the tea brought ashore so the protest could go ahead to its ultimate conclusion: a showdown with the governor and Parliament.

"Who's the master of the *Dartmouth*?" Mr. Adams asked.

"Captain Hall," Mr. Hancock answered promptly.

"Send word to Captain Hall that he is to bring his ship in at once. Who will draft a note?"

Dr. Church volunteered. Oliver felt a tingle of excitement. He would probably be asked to write the note.

"What will be done with the tea when it arrives?" another man wanted to know.

"Burn it, ship and all!" suggested William Molineux.

"Absolutely not!" Dr. Warren, seated beside Dr. Church, rose to his feet. "We want no *Gaspee*s here. The tea is the target, not the *Dartmouth*."

Oliver's face burned at the mention of the torched schooner. The liberty men of Providence were no bolder than the men of Boston, but the *Gaspee* wasn't guarded by a fort and several British ships of war. Dr. Warren's wisdom eased Oliver's fears.

"I think we can leave the final disposition of the tea to a later meeting," Paul Revere said. "We must alert the people first. Mr. Edes, do you have the new handbill?"

Benjamin Edes of the Loyal Nine stood up with a slip of paper in his hand. He read: "Friends! Brethren! Countrymen! That worst of plagues, the detested tea, shipped for this port by the East India Company, is now arrived in this harbor; the hour of destruction or manly oppositions to the machinations of tyranny stares you in the face; every friend to his country, to himself, and posterity is now called upon to meet at Faneuil Hall at nine o' clock this day,"—by which he meant tomorrow, November 29—"to make a united and successful resistance to this last, worst, and most destructive measure of administration."

"Here! Here!" the men cried, thumping the table to express their approval. With a bow, Mr. Edes sat down. His print shop would flood the city with leaflets before morning.

Dr. Warren and Dr. Church next presented their own handbill, intended for the towns surrounding Boston, urging like-minded patriots to attend the Faneuil Hall meeting. Mr. Revere promised his network of messengers would get the notices to the countryside as soon as the ink on them was dry.

Before the meeting was done, a boy burst up the stairs, red faced from running. He'd come from the harbor, he announced, well out of breath. A signal from the *Dartmouth* had been relayed to shore. The committee had a friend on board the tea ship (Oliver heard the name "Hodgdon" whispered) who managed to signal remarkable news. Two royal customs officers had boarded the *Dartmouth* at Castle William!

The room exploded.

"What does it mean?" Oliver asked Dr. Church.

"The tea has been officially received," the doctor said through the uproar. "Now it can never go back, not without violating the Acts of Trade, which our dear governor would never do." Without meaning to, royal officials had delivered to the Sons of Liberty the cause they needed.

The next day more than five thousand people showed up for the meeting, too many for Faneuil Hall. To accommodate the crowd, the gathering was moved to Old South Church. People came from all around Boston—Cambridge, Dorchester, Charlestown, and Roxbury. The new assembly passed resounding resolutions that the tea should not be landed in Massachusetts, no tax would ever be paid on it, and the most hated beverage should be returned to England immediately.

The tea merchants fled to Castle William. The committee was unhappy about this. Samuel Adams wanted to capture and hold the tea merchants as ransom against the tea, but a timely warning allowed the merchants to escape. Someone who knew the workings of the committee had talked.

"We'll have them, we'll have them," Oliver heard Adams mutter. He wondered just who Adams meant, the merchants or the informer?

When the great meeting at Old South Church reconvened, the owner of the *Dartmouth*, Mr. Rotch, and Captain Hall, were there. The assembly ordered Hall to bring his ship to a wharf at once. A special band of volunteer watchmen would safeguard the ship and prevent the tea from being taken off. Having no choice, Captain Hall agreed.

At this point, one of Samuel Adams's close friends, Dr. Thomas Young, declared loudly, "The only way to get rid of the tea is to throw it overboard!"

The meeting was not yet ready to sanction violence. Enough people present felt sympathy for the tea merchants and shipowners not to destroy the cargo and property of honest businessmen.

Dr. Church, seated down front with other members of the committee, beckoned Oliver to him. Oliver walked over and knelt by the doctor's chair.

"I cannot leave now, but this message must be delivered," he murmured. With great care he slipped a small square of paper into Oliver's hand. "Go to my house and wait there. A man will call for the note. Give it to him and ask no questions."

Oliver gave his employer a curious glance. Dr. Church said, "Special business of the committee, understand?" Oliver nodded and slipped out of the church.

It was clear and blustery outside, and growing colder. Oliver put the paper in his shoe and hurried to Dr. Church's home. The empty house was very still. Lily and Hilde were in Raynham with Dr. Church's family. Horatio Beebe had remained at Old South Church with the doctor's carriage.

Oliver let himself in the back door. He tracked through the scullery and hall to the doctor's front room. From there he could see the street.

He sat in the dim room, waiting. A clock on the mantle ticked loudly until it ran down and suddenly stopped. The silence was like a bell ringing. Oliver turned to look at the expired timepiece. It was five minutes past five o' clock.

The paper in his shoe nagged at him. He tried to ignore it, but it grew unbearable. Digging it out, Oliver found it was sealed with a bit of gum.

Special business of the committee? That made no sense. The whole committee was in Old South Church. Who could the doctor be writing to? Thoughts of Mrs. Lemon and gold sovereigns kept turning up in his head.

In the scullery, Oliver found a chafing dish, used to keep dishes warm, away from the kitchen. He scrounged up a kettle and set it on the dish. Flame licked the bottom of the pot. Before long a feather of steam was jetting from the kettle's spout. Oliver held the paper in the steam. The seal softened. Oliver deftly unfolded the paper and spread it out. By the light of the chafing dish he read:

*All resolved to force a fight. Tea will be destroyed not sent
back not paid for. Suspect attack on ships at anchor. Send
frigates to guard. Put marines on ships. Attack will be
soon. Take all care. B. C.*

Send frigates? Marines on the tea ships? Who was Dr.
Church giving advice to, the redcoats?

There was a knock on the front door. Oliver hastily
refolded the paper. The gum would not stick. More knocking
forced him to forget the seal. He rushed to the front door.

A man in a long cloak stood there. The stock at his throat
was as white as a full moon.

"You have something for me?" He held out his right hand.

Mutely, Oliver put the paper in the man's gloved hand. He
plainly saw the paper was curled open.

"Anything I should tell the doctor?" Oliver asked
nervously.

The man turned away in a swirl of black cloak. Though he
only said a few words, Oliver had recognized him right
enough. The visitor was Captain Cane, the redcoat officer who
saved Oliver from the angry soldiers some weeks ago.

Oliver did not sleep that night. He got up early and went
looking for someone to confide his suspicions to. Finding Dr.
Warren, he suddenly felt reluctant. Dr. Warren and Dr. Church
were colleagues and friends. How much did one doctor know
about the other? How far would Dr. Warren go to defend his
friend?

His next choice was Mr. Revere. He had always been kind to Oliver, and no one in Boston had a greater reputation for dependability than Paul Revere.

He asked Dr. Warren where Mr. Revere might be.

"He's likely at his shop," Dr. Warren replied. Noting the young man's nervousness, he said, "Can I help you, Carter?"

"No, sir, thank you." Oliver hurried off to Paul Revere's silversmithy.

Despite all the excitement about the tea shipment, Oliver found Mr. Revere hard at work supervising the casting of a silver urn. His apprentices did the hot work, and when the blisteringly hot crucible was cleared away, Oliver stepped forward.

"Carter, how are you?" Revere said idly. When Oliver didn't answer right away, Mr. Revere looked again more closely. "What has happened?"

"May I speak to you alone, sir?"

Mr. Revere led him to a storeroom. Here the shelves were lined with creamers and trays, potbellied teapots and tableware wrought in bright silver. Mr. Revere shut the door.

"Is there news from the harbor?" he said in a low voice.

"No, sir." Oliver struggled to begin. "Sir, do you trust everyone on the committee?"

Fixing him with his steady gaze, Paul Revere said, "No, I do not."

Oliver let out the breath he'd been holding. "Neither do I!" Quickly the words tumbled out. He told Mr. Revere about

Dr. Church, Mrs. Lemon, the gold sovereigns, and the message picked up by a redcoat officer. Revere listened gravely.

"You gave the note to this Captain Cane?" Oliver nodded. "Then we have no proof of Church's communication."

"You believe me, don't you?"

Mr. Revere held a finger to his lips. "Completely, lad. For some time we've known the redcoats were getting information from inside our secret councils. I suspected—" He stopped himself. "I suspected someone other than Dr. Church. But I believe you, Carter. Dr. Church is just the sort to sell us out. He loves money and pleasure, and it sounds like he is trading our secrets for British gold."

"Do you think Mrs. Lemon is a spy, too?"

"She's probably his paymaster. He could hardly collect it from the redcoats in person."

Revere paced up and down in the short room. "We can't simply confront him, not without proof. It's only your word against his." Church's family was an old and renowned one in Boston. Few would believe a charge of treason against him by a young journeyman from out of town.

Mr. Revere said, "You're close to him, Carter. Will you help us trap him?"

This was not the question Oliver expected. Dr. Church had been good to him. It was hard enough to denounce him to Mr. Revere. He was not prepared to spy on him.

"You need not agree," Revere said. "Spying is no work for decent men. It's enough you warned me about Church. I'll have a word with a few others. We'll keep an eye on the good doctor."

Oliver felt like he had failed Mr. Revere. As the silversmith went to the door, Oliver blurted out, "I will do it!"

"Are you sure? Treachery is not an easy thing to stomach."

Oliver squared his shoulders. "I will do it, sir."

Mr. Revere clapped him on the shoulder. "Good! Go back to work. Be as usual as you can. Keep your eyes and ears open, and I'll speak to you again on this matter. If something important comes up—evidence we can use against Church—find me at once." Oliver vowed he would.

On December 2, the second tea ship, *Eleanor*, arrived. *Dartmouth* had been brought to the city and moored at Griffin's Wharf, at the foot of Fort Hill. Captain Bruce of the *Eleanor* was given the same orders as Captain Hall: No tea was to be landed. All other cargo could be taken off, but the tea was not to touch Boston soil. A company of armed guards was posted on the wharf to "protect" the tea ships. In fact, the men were there to see the tea was not unloaded.

The third tea ship, *Beaver*, commanded by Captain Hezekiah Coffin, arrived December 8. As several members of *Beaver*'s crew had come down with smallpox during the voyage, the committee sent word the tea was to be brought up on deck and aired while the ship's crew was quarantined.

When this was done, the *Beaver* joined the other two ships tied up at Griffin's Wharf.

During those days, Dr. Church returned to his amiable self. He paid Oliver's wages promptly, and he offered to advance him a sum if Oliver needed it. The doctor said he could bring Hilde back from Raynham so Oliver could see her. Though he did not want Hilde anywhere near the doctor now, Oliver acted true to his instructions from Mr. Revere and gladly accepted Dr. Church's offer.

"Excellent!" the doctor declared. "I'll send Beebe for her Thursday morning."

That would be December 16, less than a week away.

chapter twelve

Invitation to a Party

On December 8, Governor Hutchinson, no longer in control of Boston, asked Admiral Montagu for help. The governor imagined Boston's patriots would try to force the tea ships to return to England. He asked Admiral Montagu to prevent this. Accordingly, the admiral moved his flagship *Captain* and two frigates into position to block any ships leaving Boston Harbor. Neither Montagu nor Hutchinson understood the Americans' intentions. Samuel Adams and the Committee of Correspondence were not going to let the tea land, nor were they going to let it go. News arrived from Philadelphia and New York that the tea importers there had resigned. Everyone in the colonies now watched to see what would happen in Boston.

On Monday, December 13, Oliver opened the dispensary as usual. Dr. Church arrived promptly at eight o'clock, looking dapper in a new satin suit. The committee was still meeting at Faneuil Hall in secret session. During a lull between patients,

Oliver asked Dr. Church why he wasn't at the hall with his colleagues.

"I shall attend later today," said the doctor. "This morning I must make some coin! Are you afraid they will take action without you?"

"Well . . . yes, sir."

"Fear not," Dr. Church said cheerfully. "Soon there will be a tea party the likes of which Boston has never seen!"

Dr. Church remained until mid-afternoon, then he closed his casebook and bid Oliver good day. Oliver had a pile of prescriptions to prepare, some of them very elaborate. As he labored on them past sunset, it occurred to him the doctor might have deliberately given him difficult prescriptions just to keep him busy.

Beebe had already left for Raynham with the carriage. Dr. Church promised he would return on Friday with Hilde.

Oliver was not allowed into the closed session of the committee. Recent leaks to the authorities made it very clear someone was betraying the Americans' plans. Only the most trusted members of the committee were admitted. Oliver languished outside.

While he cooled his heels, word came *Beaver* was headed for Griffin's Wharf to tie up with the other tea ships. The fourth tea ship, the brigantine *William*, ran into a gale off Cape Cod and was wrecked. That was one ship the committee didn't have to worry about.

Oliver was summoned to Dr. Church's house on the evening of the fifteenth. It was very windy and cold. Wrapped up in his long coat, Oliver reached Hanover Street an hour after sundown. The front room lamps were lit, and three carriages were drawn up in front of the doctor's house. Oliver went to the front door and knocked. Dr. Church answered the door himself.

"Carter! Just the fellow we need!" he said brightly. "Come on inside!"

In the front room were Dr. Warren and Dr. Williams, fellow physicians and members of the committee. They were drinking sherry and reading aloud the minutes of the meeting at Faneuil Hall. The doctors stopped reading when Oliver joined them.

"Here's the man for your errand, Joseph," said Dr. Church.

"Carter? Yes, he'll do." Dr. Warren put aside his papers. "You know what burned cork is, Carter?"

"Yes, sir. It's a pigment used to blacken ointments."

"Correct. We need a supply of burned cork, right away."

Oliver had an ounce or so at the dispensary. He mentioned this to the doctors. They laughed.

"We need a good deal more than that!" said Dr. Church. "More like twenty pounds."

Oliver must have looked completely baffled. Dr. Church explained.

"We need a quantity that will disguise a sizable body of men," he said.

Oliver's heart beat faster. There was to be action!

"It will take me three days to compound that much ointment if I do nothing else," he said.

"We don't have three days," said Dr. Williams, frowning. "We need it tomorrow." Oliver protested, but Dr. Church came to his rescue.

"One of my patients, Joshua Bradshaw, has a warehouse by Gray's Wharf," he said. "He assures me he has a hogshead of burned cork stored there." He chuckled. "He sells quite a lot of it to the Indians of Upper Canada. They paint themselves with it."

"Now he can sell it to members of a local tribe," Dr. Warren said with a straight face. All three men burst out laughing.

Dr. Church gave Oliver directions to Gray's Wharf. He told him to go there tomorrow afternoon between four and five o' clock. He was to get the barrel of burned cork and take it to the Green Dragon.

"Tell no one what you do, and make sure you're not observed along the way," Dr. Church said. He ushered Oliver to the front door.

"Do I need any money for the cork?" asked Oliver on the front step.

"I'll settle with Bradshaw," said Dr. Church. "Be of good cheer, lad! Your sweetheart will be here tomorrow. Keep thinking of her. That will put wings in your heels!"

Thursday, December 16, dawned rainy and cold. Today the duty had to be paid, or the tea returned to England. Because a decision had to come today, another public meeting was scheduled at Old South Church that morning. People flooded the building beyond its capacity. Almost seven thousand were there, a third of whom were from towns outside Boston. The owners of the tea ships appeared before the committee, but they had nothing new to say. Governor Hutchinson would not allow the return of the tea unless the duty was paid, nor would he allow it to simply rot in the anchored ships.

As darkness fell, the assembly waited for one last report from Francis Rotch, owner of the *Dartmouth*. Rotch had traveled all the way to Milton, Massachusetts, where Governor Hutchinson had gone to avoid Boston's angry mobs. Rotch got no help from the governor. Before he left on his errand to retrieve the cork for the Sons of Liberty, Oliver heard this exchange:

"Will you send your vessel back with the tea in her under these present circumstances?" Rotch was asked.

"I cannot possibly do so," he said. "It would prove my absolute ruin."

Rotch was next questioned about his intention to land the tea. The doughty shipowner considered.

"I have no business doing so, but if I were called upon to do so by the proper persons, I would try to land it for my own security's sake," he said.

A man in the audience cried, "Who knows how tea will mingle with seawater?"

The crowd roared with approval. Some chanted, "A mob! A mob!" The moderator of the meeting, Mr. Savage, quieted the excited crowd.

At this point, Oliver slipped out. It was only a matter of time now before action was taken.

A little past sundown he made his way to Gray's Wharf. He took the waterfront road, passing right by Griffin's Wharf on the way. The tea ships were tied up to the dock, guarded by a company of volunteers. The meeting in Old South Church was still going strong when he reached Bradshaw's warehouse. It was a low, rambling building fronting directly on the water. Judging by the rusty door hinges, not a lot of commerce went on there. Through a dirty window, Oliver saw a gleam of light inside. He knocked carefully on a side door. After a long time, he heard a bolt being drawn back. The door squeaked open a few inches.

"Whozzat?" slurred a voice.

"My name's Carter. Dr. Church sent me."

The unseen man cleared his throat. "In with you, then." He hauled the door open further. Oliver ducked inside.

The air within smelled strongly of mold. A narrow path led through lines of crates and barrels to a cleared space where a lone candle burned. Snorting loudly, the man led Oliver to the dim light.

"Where's the burned cork?" Oliver asked, not liking his surroundings much. He wanted to get what he came for and go quickly.

"Over here."

The path through the crates ended at a small table where the candle burned. The flame did not flicker at all, the air was so still. Seated at the table in a dusty greatcoat was a man with rusty brown hair and bushy eyebrows. He was drinking from a squat bottle of rum.

Oliver's guide turned to him. He was close in age to his companion, with yellow hair starting to whiten with age. There was something familiar about these two, something about the pair of them together—

"So where is it?" Oliver asked.

The seated man stood up. He drew a short wooden club from his coat pocket.

"Right here."

Oliver turned to run. The second man tried to grab him from behind. Oliver hit him solidly in the chin with his elbow and broke free. The first man landed a glancing blow on Oliver's head that blotted out his vision for a moment. He stumbled away, hit the table, and knocked the candle over. The light went out.

The men cursed loudly. Their oaths helped Oliver recognize them at last: the two redcoats who came to Dr. Church's dispensary all those months ago when one of them had a broken arm!

"Jack, where is he?" said one of the soldiers.

"By the table, I think."

Oliver crawled on his hands and knees, trying to find the gap in the crates that led to the door. Instead he bumped into one of the redcoats. The man grabbed him, punching Oliver with his fist.

"I got him, Tommy! Right here!"

The second man fell on Oliver, and he went to the floor with both redcoats on top of him.

"Tie his hands," said Tommy. Rough ship's cord was wrapped tightly around Oliver's wrists.

Jack relit the candle. Oliver was hauled up to a sitting position. Blood ran down his lip.

"Why are you doing this?" Oliver gasped. "What harm have I done you?"

"Not us, lad. We owe a favor to a certain gentleman. He wants you out."

"Out of Boston?"

Tommy laughed. "Out of this world!"

Oliver coughed. He tasted blood. "You mean Dr. Church, don't you?"

"You best not speak any names, if you want to keep any of your teeth."

Jack dragged over a large canvas sack. Oliver watched closely, knowing the bag was meant for him.

"I'll be missed!" he said. "The committee knows about Dr. Church's treachery—if I disappear, they'll know he had a hand in it!"

"That's the chance he takes, innit?" Tommy looked around for something. "Where's the bloody rope, Jack?"

"I haven't got it."

"Lovely! How are we going to tie the bag shut without rope? Find some!"

Jack moved off in the shadows, searching for rope. Oliver slowly gathered his feet under him. Next time Tommy turned his back—

Oliver leaped to his feet, lowered his head, and butted the redcoat in the small of the back. Tommy flew over the table, snuffing the candle again, and landing with a crash against a crate. Oliver had oriented himself before the light went out, and he found the way out despite the pitch darkness. He made it to the door, kicked it open, only to find someone in his way: Dr. Church's coachman.

"Beebe!" he cried. "Help me! Dr. Church wants me dead!"

Smiling benignly, Beebe took Oliver's arm in an iron grip.

"What the doctor wants, the doctor shall have," he said pleasantly. "That's the hard price you pay for reading other chaps' mail."

"Beebe!"

"Sergeant Beebe, if you please. Late of His Majesty's dragoons."

He shoved Oliver back inside. Jack and Tommy had the candle burning again. They glared at Oliver ferociously, tired of chasing him around.

"Let's kill him now!" said Jack, displaying a long knife.

"No, no," said Beebe. "You did that to Brown, and it nearly ruined everything. Young Mr. Carter must vanish. That way our employer can deflect any suspicion from himself."

"Why did you kill Ezekiel Brown?" Oliver said. "Wasn't he working for you?"

"Lord, no! He was spying on the doctor for your damned committee. Kind of you to let Dr. Church know about him," Beebe said.

Oliver was forced into a chair. His pulse pounded. Poor Brown, slain by Oliver's misguided zeal. If only someone had warned him who Brown worked for! These secret doings were too much for him. Now one liberty man was dead, and it looked like he would be joining him.

Beebe kept Oliver quiet by laying the barrel of a cocked pistol on his shoulder. Jack and Tommy fumbled with the canvas bag until the sergeant snapped at them to cease.

"Find a weight," Beebe said calmly. "Something you can tie to his feet. Understand?"

"Don't kill me," Oliver said. His tongue felt like it was coated with glue. "I'll go away and never come back. I've done it before."

"You're a proper lad, I can see that," Beebe said. "But orders is orders. Dr. Church is already under suspicion. Once you're gone, he can go back to being a loyal Son of Liberty and informing General Haldimand on everything your radical friends do."

The soldiers returned with a length of heavy ship's chain. At Beebe's direction, they wrapped it around Oliver's ankles as tightly as possible.

"Don't just stand there," Beebe barked. "Pick him up! He can't walk out on his own!"

Jack grabbed Oliver under the arms. Tommy hoisted his feet. With much grunting they hauled him out a seaside door. A small rowboat was tied to the pier.

"He might yell," Jack remarked.

Beebe studied Oliver and smiled benignly. "That he might." He stuffed a not-very-clean kerchief from his pocket in Oliver's mouth.

"Farewell, lad. All the pill rollers in Boston will miss you. So will that little German girl, eh?"

Up to that moment, Oliver had been scared—scared to death. Mention of Hilde made him angry. Not only did he love her, but the idea that she would have to labor on under Mrs. Church's thumb made his blood boil. He grew even angrier thinking about Dr. Church. Wretched traitor, he sold out his friends and fellow Americans so he could afford fine clothes and keep a grand house.

Jack climbed in the boat and moved forward. Oliver was prodded in, falling hard on his knees. He groaned against his gag. Tommy got down and held the oars while Beebe cast off the line.

"Take him where's it is deep, lads," he said. "Past South Battery, at least."

Hardly had he said that when the sound of distant shouting reached them. It was far away, but it was loud enough to be the voice of a sizable crowd.

The tea! The speeches and wrangling were over. The patriots were going to get rid of the hated tea!

Beebe understood, too. He tucked his pistol away inside his heavy cape. "The fools are after the company's tea," he said, gazing in the direction of Griffin's Wharf. "There will be hell to pay this night."

He pushed off the boat with his foot. Jack lowered the oars and started rowing. Oliver rolled to a sitting position facing Tommy in the stern. When they cleared the end of Gray's Wharf, they saw torches filling Griffin's dock. There was no shooting or sounds of a struggle.

Several hundred patriots had come to the waterfront. True to what the doctors had told Oliver, many of them had their faces blackened with cork. They stuck feathers in their hair and waved hatchets, pretending to be Indians. No one was fooled, but the face paint and feathers hid the identity of many of the raiders.

The thousand-strong mob quickly took over the ships. One by one, the hatches on the *Dartmouth*, *Beaver*, and *Eleanor* were removed, and chests of tea taken out on deck. The tea chests were opened. Hundreds and hundreds of pounds of dry Bohea tea were dumped overboard. When all the tea had been disposed of, the raiders returned the empty chests to the hold, swept the deck clean, and left the ships as tidy as they had found them.

Drifting with the tide, Oliver and his captors watched with amazement as the valuable cargo (estimated to be worth 10,000 pounds sterling) was flung into the sea. The tide was slack, and drifts of soggy tea covered the water.

Shaking off his fascination with the scene, Oliver managed to slip his feet free of the heavy chain. The soldiers had wrapped it tightly around his ankles but did not lock or tie the links in place.

Hearing the chain clink, Jack said, "Be still you!"

"Why don't we dump him here?" Tommy asked. "I'm tired of rowing through this muck."

"I'm the one doing the work around here," Jack retorted. He shifted, and the boat rocked. Tommy was on his feet watching the tea party unfold half a mile away. He objected when Jack rocked the boat.

I'll rock you, Oliver thought, seething. Once his feet were free he leaped up, chewing hard on his gag. He got it in one cheek and succeeded in spitting it out.

"He's up!"

Jack let go of the oars and lunged with his knife. Oliver flung himself backward, colliding hard with Tommy. The boat swung wildly, then dumped all three of them into the frigid water.

Oliver sank. His hands were still tied behind his back. He bent double, trying to work his wrists over his hips and feet. It was black as tar underwater and deadly cold. Fortunately, Oliver had already wrung some slack from the rope, and he managed to work his hands free. Oliver kicked to the surface.

He burst upward, gasping. Instead of air he got a mass of soggy tea leaves plastered to his face. Down he sank. Oliver swam underwater a few yards and tried to surface. Again he was hampered by a heavy layer of sodden Bohea tea. He had escaped his enemies, but he was foundering anyway—drowning under a blanket of slick, wet tea.

Wiping his face to get rid of the clinging leaves, Oliver tried to swim on the surface. Tea stuck to his eyes, ears, and nose. When he tried to draw breath, he choked on the stuff. Oliver glanced back. The rowboat had capsized. One man was hanging on—he couldn't tell which one—but there was no sign of the other.

With no other choice, Oliver dove. He swam away from the wharves, trying desperately to find open water. Lungs burning, he popped up in the ship channel. Several vessels were anchored there. He could see their lamps burning.

His legs were going numb. Unable to kick, Oliver began to sink. He paddled furiously with his hands, but the killing cold crept through his body.

"Help!" he cried feebly. "Help!"

He tried to float on his back, but he was so fouled with tea and wet clothing that he sank again. Oliver struggled back to the surface and called for help one last time.

He heard the thump and squeak of oarlocks. His mind reeled. He imagined Tommy and Jack had righted the boat and were after him. With the dark shape of a boat looming over him, he struck at the hands trying to take hold of him.

"Easy, lad, easy," a voice said.

He was seized by many hands. Overcome by exhaustion and cold, Oliver collapsed unconscious in the bottom of a longboat.

chapter thirteen

Prison in the Sun

F ar away, great waters were moving. Oliver heard them, and he tried to rouse himself from the deep sleep that bound his body like ropes and chains.

Ropes and chains!

Oliver sat up abruptly, banging his head on a low beam. He was in a narrow bunk under heavy blankets. The bunk rolled and plunged. It took him a long time to realize he was belowdecks on a ship.

His first thoughts were: Dr. Church—the attack on the tea ships—treachery! Throwing back the blanket, he found he was wearing the same clothes he had on when he went to Bradshaw's warehouse. They smelled of tea and salt water.

Oliver climbed down. The deck heaved under him, almost dropping him on his knees. Boston Harbor was never this rough unless a hurricane was roaring through. What was going on? Where could he have been taken?

150

He staggered to a nearby ladder. Sunshine stabbed his eyes. Cold wind whirled and eddied through the open hatch. Unsure of his footing, Oliver mounted the rungs slowly.

On deck, he was amazed to see he was no longer in Boston harbor, but sailing briskly on the open sea. The ship was a small brigantine. A sailor spotted him blinking at the top of the open hatch. He shouted for the captain.

A stern-looking man of fifty appeared. His cocked hat was tied on with a woolen scarf.

"You live, sir! Glad to know it. God has preserved you after a great trial!"

"Who are you?" Oliver managed to say. His voice sounded like the creak of a rusty hinge.

"Gideon Ashworth, master of the good ship *Golightly*, on which you stand."

Oliver looked out to sea. All he could see to the horizon were white-capped waves.

"Where are we, Captain?"

"Off the Jersey coast. This glorious wind, which God has given us, has driven us far in half a day."

Captain Ashworth explained his men had fished Oliver out of Boston harbor half drowned and nearly dead from cold. They cleaned the soggy tea from his face, dosed him with rum, and put him in a bunk to recover—or die. It was late afternoon of the next day, December 17.

Oliver was appalled. While heartily glad to be alive, he couldn't do anything he needed to do from the deck of the bounding brig, speeding south past New Jersey. He asked how soon he could get back to Boston.

"I can't say, sir," Ashworth replied. "If this fine wind lasts, we might reach our destination in ten days."

"What is your destination, Captain?"

"Kingston, sir, the port of Jamaica."

The captain's response horrified Oliver. Had Dr. Church meant for him to be kidnapped he couldn't have arranged it better. He tried in vain to convince Captain Ashworth to return to Boston immediately.

"Can't be done, sir. I have a cargo I must deliver as soon as God's wind and tide allow me." He surveyed the brilliant blue sky, swept clear of clouds. "Even if I wanted to, I couldn't beat to windward a mile against this blow. No, sir, we're bound for Jamaica."

The wind died on the third day out, slowing *Golightly* to a crawl. Instead of ten days to Kingston, it took sixteen. When Oliver went ashore at last, he sought paper and pen to write urgent letters to Paul Revere and Hilde. He wrote half a dozen letters and posted them with ships going back to New England. Oliver wanted to go himself, but he could not afford the passage.

He had arrived in Jamaica with exactly eight pence in his pocket. Captain Ashworth generously offered to hire Oliver as his ship's doctor, but he was not going back to Boston. *Golightly*'s next port of call was Bristol, England.

Oliver found work at a dispensary in Kingston. It was run by a minister of the Church of England, a staunch Tory named Houghton. When newspapers arrived with the story of the tea ships in Boston, Oliver knew the fight for American liberty had truly begun. As punishment for the destruction of the tea, Parliament closed the port of Boston with the Coercive Acts.

No ships could come to or go from Boston until the lost tea was paid for and the culprits responsible for dumping it were punished. The other colonies responded by sending food, fuel, and fodder to the embattled Bostonians.

Early in the new year 1774, Oliver learned it would be unwise for him to return to Boston even when he could buy passage. According to official accounts in the newspapers, the authorities in Massachusetts were hunting for the author of some intimidating letters sent to royal officials and tea merchants. The writer was only known by the initials, O.C.

Oliver read those lines twice. He understood now that Dr. Church had used Oliver's initials, not as a joke, but to give himself a useful scapegoat. Worse, copies of the *Boston Gazette*, printed outside the city and smuggled abroad in packing crates, hinted that a traitor to American liberty had been "discovered too late, having escaped by ship to the South." Beebe's remark that Dr. Church would use Oliver's absence to blacken his name with the Sons of Liberty was true. If Oliver's letters had reached Boston, his words had gone unheeded. Nowhere did the papers mention any exposure of

Dr. Church. Apparently he continued to enjoy the trust of liberty men in Boston.

Unable to return and face prison or hanging, Oliver toiled on in Jamaica. The Caribbean sun baked the New England cold from his bones, and he grew lean and sinewy from his labors. He wrote regularly to Mr. Revere, to Dr. Warren, and to John Avery. None were ever answered. He also wrote to Hilde, pledging he would return someday soon and begging her not to believe any of the stories that might be circulating about him.

Oliver lingered in the tropics for another year. One day in the spring of 1775, Oliver was in his workshop, grinding cinchona bark for fever pills when he heard the news. War had broken out in the colonies! American militia had resisted the redcoats when they tried to march from Boston to Concord to seize the colonists' supplies of powder and guns. They also tried to arrest John Hancock and Samuel Adams, but both men evaded capture.

At Lexington, the militia traded musket fire with the redcoats, and Americans had died defying the rule of tyranny. When the redcoats marched back to Boston, a rising storm of American militia dogged their steps, sniping at the ordered ranks from every bush and fence. This went on all day until the exhausted redcoats could stand no more. They bolted back to Boston, where they were now besieged by ten thousand outraged American militiamen.

Oliver sought out Rector Houghton and resigned on the spot. With his small savings he ran to the docks to buy passage on the first ship back to New England. With war in the air, no captain was eager to sail into danger. The closest passage Oliver could arrange was to New Bern, North Carolina. With all his worldly belongings packed in a simple haversack, Oliver boarded the ship *Mary Glance* for the mainland.

It didn't matter now if the British thought he wrote the O.C. letters. Hostilities were a fact. Once he got home, he would expose Dr. Church for the wretched turncoat he was.

And then he would find Hilde.

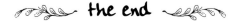

the end

The Real History Behind the Story

Benjamin Church was born August 24, 1734, in Newport, Rhode Island. His grandfather (also named Benjamin) was a renowned soldier who fought the French and Indians in King Philip's War (1676). Dr. Church graduated from Harvard in 1754. He studied medicine in America and in London. While pursuing his medical studies in England, he met and married Hannah Hill.

Dr. Church returned to America and set up practice. He was by all accounts a good physician. He was also a talented speaker and writer, abilities he lent to the growing liberty movement in the American colonies. In his writing, Dr. Church mocked Parliament's policies and the king's clumsy ministers. Later it was noticed, with a few name changes, his clever satires worked just as well

Dr. Church wrote a famous speech about the Boston Massacre of 1770. This engraving of the tragic event was done by Paul Revere.

against the opponents of the king and Parliament.

Dr. Church did write a famous speech about the Boston Massacre of 1770. He also acted as the city coroner, examining the bodies of the slain.

A Traitor

Just what led this talented man to betray his friends and countrymen is unknown. The usual theory is that Dr. Church was deeply in debt. He spent beyond his means, trying to live the life of an eighteenth-century gentleman even though he did not have the funds to do so. Among his many extravagances was his second home in Raynham, Massachusetts.

Dr. Benjamin Church played an important role in the liberty movement in the colonies before betraying his country to help the British.

If Dr. Church's need for money drove him to inform, it never seems to have troubled his conscience. In all his surviving testimony, the doctor maintained his innocence. He claimed he took British gold while sending false and misleading information in return, to dishearten the redcoats. By the time he was unmasked in 1775, no one believed this argument.

The letters signed "O.C., Sec'y" were real. They were most likely written by John Avery of the Loyal Nine and signed with whatever random initials the patriots needed.

Paul Revere actually did suspect Dr. Church for a long time, but he could not prove Church was the source of the information leak to the British. Dr. Church was finally caught almost two years after the "Tea Party" when secret messages he wrote to Major Cane (a real officer) fell into American hands. Dr. Church wrote the message in a simple substitution cipher. Three patriots—Reverend Samuel West,

Elbridge Gerry, and militia colonel Elisha Porter—decoded Church's cipher message.

Dr. Church's Fate

Dr. Church was convicted of treasonable correspondence with the enemy. It was commonly assumed at the time he would be hanged—the usual punishment for spies—but the Continental Congress discovered it had not passed any laws making espionage a capital crime. Unable to legally hang Dr. Church, he was kept in jail in Norwich, Connecticut. He was so hated by Massachusetts patriots that on one occasion they broke into his jail to kill him. Dr. Church escaped the mob by jumping out a window, but he was soon rounded up and confined again. Another gang broke into the Church house and stripped it of everything of value.

The doctor languished in jail until 1780, when Congress amended his sentence to permanent exile. He boarded a schooner commanded by a Captain Smithwick, and sailed for the West Indies. The schooner was lost with all hands somewhere at sea. Hannah Church, abandoned by her husband and destitute, managed to scrape up enough money to buy passage back to England.

Almost two years after the Boston Tea Party, Dr. Church was convicted of treason.

Further Reading

Fiction

Elliott, L. M. *Give Me Liberty*. New York: HarperCollins Publishers, 2006.

Harlow, Joan Hiatt. *Midnight Rider*. New York: Margaret K. McElderry Books, 2005.

Maxwell, Ruth H. *Eighteen Roses Red: A Young Girl's Heroic Mission in the Revolutionary War*. Shippensburg, Pa.: White Mane Kids, 2006.

Nonfiction

Allen, Thomas B. *George Washington, Spymaster: How the Americans Outspied the British and Won the Revolutionary War*. Washington, D.C.: National Geographic, 2004.

Dell, Pamela. *Benedict Arnold: From Patriot to Traitor*. Minneapolis, Minn.: Compass Point Books, 2005.

Fleming, Thomas. *Everybody's Revolution: A New Look at the People Who Won America's Freedom*. New York: Scholastic Nonfiction, 2006.

Fradin, Dennis Brindell. *The Boston Tea Party*. New York: Marshall Cavendish Benchmark, 2007.

Miller, Brandon Marie. *Declaring Independence: Life During the American Revolution*. Minneapolis, Minn.: Lerner Publications Company, 2005.

Internet Addresses

Boston Tea Party Ships and Museum
<http://www.bostonteapartyship.com/index.asp>

Colonial Williamsburg: "Spy Letter from Benjamin Church"
<http://www.cwf.org/history/teaching/enewsletter/volume3/
    january05/primsource.cfm>

Spy Letters of the American Revolution
<http://www.si.umich.edu/spies/>